MISADVENTURES

OF A

GOOD WIFE

BY
MEREDITH WILD & HELEN HARDT

MISADVENTURES

OF A

GOOD WIFE

BY
MEREDITH WILD & HELEN HARDT

WATERHOUSE PRESS

*For Helen— Thank you for being there
with me from day one!*

*For Meredith and Jon— Thank you for your
friendship, generosity, and loyalty.*

CHAPTER ONE

KATE

He always said I had the most beautiful blue eyes he'd ever seen.

In truth, my eyes were more gray than blue, but when he looked into them, his face between my thighs, his own eyes searing in their dark intensity, I believed my eyes were blue and beautiful.

"You like that, sweetness?" His words whispered across my wet skin, sending chills through me.

Price always looked into my eyes when he went down on me. He had from the very first time we'd made love back in college. Ours had been a whirlwind romance—love at first sight, as corny as that sounds. After graduation, he'd begun his job as a day trader on Wall Street, and I'd started as a copywriter for *The New York Tribune*. With luck, we'd happened upon our quaint Brooklyn apartment— cozy and perfect.

Yes, perfect.

Perfect was how I felt every time Price licked me there, tugging on me, his low growls reverberating against the sensitive skin of my inner thighs.

And his eyes never left mine.

"God, yes," I sighed. "Yes, yes."

He flipped me over onto my hands and knees and gave one cheek of my ass a little slap.

"You have the best ass, Kate."

Shivers surged through my body. I loved it when he sucked me in this position. Already, I was on the verge. I knew it wouldn't be long until he—

"Oh!"

Two of his fingers breached my wet channel, and the convulsions began. Price had given me countless orgasms over our years together, and each one always seemed more magnificent than the last. This one was an implosion—every cell in my body coursing toward my inner core. I pushed backward, trying to force his fingers farther and deeper into me.

"That's right. Come for me, sweet Kate."

My limbs shook, my arms finally giving way until only my thighs held my ass in the air.

"I love making you come," Price said, his voice low and husky. "Do you have any idea how beautiful you look right now?"

His words made me spiral toward the peak once more.

"I can feel you, sweetness. I feel you getting ready to come again." He removed his fingers, and in an instant he was inside me.

That's all it took. I exploded around him.

"Price! My God, Price!"

"That's it, baby. I love it when you scream my name. I love to make you come." He thrust once more. "You hug me so completely, Kate. No one else... No one else in the world but you..."

I pushed my hips backward, forcing him to increase his rhythm.

Hard and fast. That's how I liked it, especially right before he left on one of his trips. He always made sure I'd think only of him while he was gone.

And I always did. He never left my thoughts.

He plunged into me more deeply and then withdrew. Though I whimpered at the loss, he flipped me over onto my back, spread my legs, and then tunneled into me.

"Look at me, Kate. I want to look into your beautiful blue eyes." Beads of sweat emerged on his brow, gluing dark strands of hair to his forehand. "You're beautiful. So beautiful." He thrust once more, groaning. "God, yeah. Feels so good."

So sensitive was I from my multiple orgasms, I felt every tiny convulsion as Price shot into me.

One day we'd make a baby together. The time wasn't right yet, but one day...

He collapsed on top of me, his body hot and slick. After a few seconds, he mumbled, "Sorry, baby," and moved to the side.

I turned toward him and brushed my lips over his. "I miss you already."

His arm was over his forehead, his eyes closed. "Me too. But it's only for a week."

I smiled and kissed him again. "A week sounds like a year to me."

He opened his eyes and turned toward me. "I know. I'll call you every day like I always do." Then he sighed. "I'd better get moving if I'm going to make that flight. An afternoon nap is just what you need. You deserve it."

The bed shifted as he got up. I wanted to stay awake until he left, but I was exhausted. I'd pulled an eighty-hour week and still managed to get home to see Price before he left. Tomorrow was Saturday. I was going to indulge in a well-deserved session of sleeping in followed by a late lunch with my bestie and then a massage.

"Love you, baby," I said, drifting off.

His words echoed back to me. "And I love you. Always."

♦ ♦ ♦ ♦

I shot up in bed. What the hell was that annoying noise?

Not my alarm. I hadn't set it. I'd only lain down for an afternoon nap.

The door buzzer. I'd been so sound asleep that I hadn't recognized the ring. I quickly grabbed my phone off the night table. Noon? Damn. I'd really been exhausted. A wave of regret swept over me. I'd wanted to say goodbye to Price when he left. He was no doubt already in Switzerland by now. I hurried into some sweats and a shirt and stumbled out of the bedroom to the front door. I opened the intercom. "Yes?"

"Mrs. Lewis? Katherine Lewis?"

I cleared my throat. "Yes."

"I'm Officer Trent Nixon, NYPD. I have...news for you. May I come up?"

My heart fell into my stomach.

Something was terribly wrong.

♦ ♦ ♦ ♦

A year later...

"Come on, Kate," Michelle, my sister-in-law, urged. "You need a vacation."

"The last year has been a vacation. I've hardly worked." I hadn't needed to. Price had left me a hefty life insurance policy. With proper investment, I'd never have to work again. Which was good, because apparently I no longer had it in me.

"That's my point. You have a promising career. A promising future."

A future without Price? No thank you. I gazed at my sister-in-law. She looked so much like him, with her dark hair and expressive eyes. She even had the same fiery spirit and determination, which she was exhibiting now. Michelle had decided I needed a tropical escape with her. A girl's trip to some remote island in the South Pacific.

I wasn't buying into it.

"You can't wallow around forever," she continued.

"I can't seem to pull myself out of this, Chelle." No truer words. How was I supposed to get over the love of my life?

She touched my forearm, no doubt trying to offer comfort but failing. "I miss him too. We all do. I understand."

She *thought* she understood. But she didn't. She was his little sister, not his soulmate. Not the woman who was supposed to bear his children—those beautiful phantom babies I'd never meet. Not the woman he should have grown old with—laughing together on a park bench, feeding pigeons, watching children play.

My lover had been snatched from me by the jaws of hell, and no one got it. No one understood.

Michelle gazed around my kitchen. "When was the last time

you cleaned? Ate a decent meal?"

Dirty dishes towered high in the sink, and the remainder of my Chinese takeout from two nights ago littered the table. I hadn't been able to choke much of it down.

I didn't answer.

"Look," Michelle said. "We're getting out of here. I'm calling a cleaning service to fumigate this place, and I'm taking you to lunch. Where you *will* eat. Then we're going shopping."

I opened my mouth to protest, but she shushed me.

"No arguments. You need clothes. Island wear." Then she dug into her purse and pulled out some papers. "Here are our e-tickets and itinerary. We leave first thing tomorrow."

◆ ◆ ◆ ◆

After a turbulent flight, a ferry ride that nearly had me retching— "You're not seasick," Michelle had said. "It's just nerves."—and a bumpy, bouncy excursion ride over roads made of actual rocks, we finally arrived at a small beachfront villa on the South Pacific island of Leiloa.

The cabbie unloaded our luggage. Michelle paid him and muttered something I didn't understand.

Once the driver was on his way, she turned to me. "So what do you think?"

"I think I have to pee." The bumps and bounces to get here had taken their toll.

"For God's sake, Kate. Look around you. It's beautiful here. The beach is straight ahead, and I hear the sunsets are amazing. This is paradise. Embrace it."

The only thing I wanted to embrace was dead and buried. I picked up my suitcase and carry-on. "Let's go inside."

Michelle shook her head and sighed. "Fine." She produced a keycard and unlocked the door. "This place is supposed to be great. Four bedrooms, full kitchen. Pool and hot tub."

"What do we need with four bedrooms?" I queried.

"Just go with it for once. Okay, Kate?"

Michelle had been a good sport, putting up with my pessimistic attitude. The least I could do was try to enjoy this trip she'd arranged. She'd obviously gone to a lot of effort. Everything had been first class all the way. It was likely costing an arm and a leg. At least I could afford it. "You win. Let's go with it."

The villa was beautiful and decorated in a plush modern style. The kitchen was equipped with a gourmet stove, marble countertops, and a huge stainless steel refrigerator.

Michelle opened it and pulled out a bottle of Moët. "Some bubbles to toast the beginning of our three weeks in paradise."

I wasn't in a partying mood quite yet. "No thank you."

"Hey. Remember? You're going to go with it." She unwrapped the cork and pulled it out with a pop.

"You're right. I said that." Trying to do my part, I searched the cupboards until I found some champagne flutes. Michelle filled them and handed one to me.

"To finding what we've lost," she said, clinking my glass.

I inhaled deeply. She'd chosen interesting words. I would never literally find what I'd lost, but maybe I could find part of myself—a part that was strong, a part that could help me get through what was coming. "All right. To finding what we've lost." I took a drink of the sparkling liquid. The bubbles danced across my tongue.

"To that end," Michelle said, "let's change clothes and go for a walk on the beach. You take the room at the end of the hallway upstairs. I'll take the bedroom down here."

I lugged my bags upstairs to the room she'd chosen for me...and dropped my jaw to the floor when I walked in. This was the master suite of all master suites. I didn't need this room. Why had she rented this particular villa, anyway? We could have made do in one hotel room with two beds.

The king-size bed was draped in black and silver silk, and the dressers and night tables were dark cherry. But that was nothing compared to the bathroom. Pure decadence. Silvery white marble countertops and black porcelain fixtures, including a bidet. The tub and steam shower were both big enough for two. I inhaled. The entire room smelled of rose and lavender.

I unpacked a few things and changed into a hot pink bikini that Michelle had insisted I buy. "You have a great body," she'd said. "Show it off!"

To whom I was going to show it off, I had no idea. I put it on anyway and wrapped a black and pink sarong around my waist. I wriggled my toes into some flip-flops, brushed out my honey-blond hair and gathered it into a high ponytail, and went back downstairs.

Michelle was waiting for me in the kitchen, dressed in a royal-blue bikini top and white broomstick skirt. She handed me another glass of champagne. "Some bubbles for the walk."

"On a public beach?"

"Silly. This is a *private* beach. Did you notice any other houses around when we drove up here?"

I hadn't noticed much of anything. I'd been too busy feeling sorry for myself. "I'm sorry. Then I guess it's okay."

"It's *all* okay," she said, smiling. "Go on out. Walk to the left. The view is spectacular. I'll catch up in a minute." She sipped her drink.

"No. I'll wait for you."

"I have a quick call to make, and I don't want you hanging around here when the beach and waves are right outside. Go. I don't want you to miss the sunset."

What did I have to lose? I'd already lost everything. Walking on the beach by myself for a few minutes wouldn't hurt me. I stepped outside, gripping the stem of my glass, and looked toward the ocean. The sun was nearing the horizon, a bright orange ball with rays of yellow and white radiating around it. It was still quite bright, so I shielded my eyes. I hadn't thought to put on sunglasses.

Then I walked along the shoreline, looking down at the myriad shells and flora that had been washed ashore. After I'd gone a few yards, I looked back for Michelle. No sign of her yet.

I continued, looking again to the sun and then ahead, when—

Michelle had said this was a private beach. So why was a figure walking toward me?

I squinted, trying to get a better look. Something seemed so familiar about the confident stride...

My heart jumped.

No.

It couldn't be.

A ghost was walking toward me.

A ghost who said I had the most beautiful blue eyes he'd ever seen.

15

CHAPTER TWO

PRICE

I'd dreamed of this day. I'd lain in bed countless nights torturing myself with the possibility of it. At least half those nights were spent trying to talk myself out of it too.

I could have let her move on and forget about me. Maybe that would have been the right thing to do, but the minute I picked up the phone and called Michelle, I knew there was no going back. Even if Kate had fallen in love with someone else, I'd find a way to get her back. She was my wife, and nothing would ever change that. Not even my supposed death.

The sun was hot on my shoulders, the sand giving way to my footsteps as I walked toward her figure on the beach. She was faced my way, her gaze seemingly fixed on me. My heart started to race. Did she recognize me already?

My imagination rushed through every scenario I'd fantasized about. Her happy tears. Jumping into my arms. Falling into bed the first second we could. My palms itched to touch her again. My sweet Kate...

She stood stock still as I approached, her mouth agape, arms limp by her sides. So no jumping into my arms then.

I slowed in front of her, and my heart stopped as our gazes locked. Those blue eyes... Heaven help me, they'd slain me the second I saw them back in school. I was a goner. Nothing had changed.

"Kate."

I reached out, desperate to touch her.

But she shook her head, lifting a trembling hand to her lips. "It can't be."

"Kate, it's me," I said with more force. "It's Price."

She kept shaking her head, almost stumbling backward. "You're not real. This isn't real. You're dead."

"No, I'm real, sweetheart. It's me. I promise you." I couldn't keep my distance anymore. I took a couple long strides toward her, grasping her arms and bringing us chest to chest.

But the second I touched her, a sob tore from her throat. Her pain was so raw, so real. It clawed down my limbs and slugged me in the gut. I wrapped my arms around her, buried my face in her neck, and breathed her in. Grapefruit. God, she still smelled the same. I wished everything else could be the same right now.

She was still sobbing, her body so delicate in my arms. She was thinner. I hadn't missed the dark circles under her eyes, either. The lifelessness that lived under the shock she wore at seeing me. I'd make all that go away...as soon as she stopped crying and let me kiss her and love her.

I hushed her, pulled back enough to see her face and brush away her tears. Then a flash of dark hair behind her caught my eye. Michelle stood on the lanai several yards away.

"Chelle."

The second I said her name she ran toward us. Kate pulled away before I could keep her close, and Michelle took the space in a flash.

"You bastard. Oh my God, I can't believe you're really here. It's really you!"

Tears flowed down her cheeks, catching on her smile and wetting my face as she peppered a thousand kisses all over me. I held her tight, and her tears soon turned into laughter. I hadn't heard such a wonderful sound since... Well, since a happier time.

She finally stepped back, and we both turned to Kate, who had wrapped her arms around herself. Despite the tropical heat, she shivered.

Michelle took her hand. "Come on. Let's go inside and finish that bottle. We have to celebrate."

Kate managed a weak smile, her gaze floating back to me like she still couldn't believe I was real. I followed them both inside, noting the open-air design of the house. Nothing like the non-stop pump of air conditioning to kill the joy of being on a temperate island.

"Beautiful place," I said with a grin. I'd picked this villa for the occasion after a little research. It had to be remote, of course, but for Kate, it also had to be the best. I hoped she liked it. Without a doubt, it beat the boat I'd called home for the past many months.

Kate leaned against the bar-height counter, a faraway look in her eyes, while Michelle bounced from the stainless steel fridge to the dark lacquered cabinets, pulling out another champagne flute.

"It's amazing. You sure know how to pick the perfect spot for a family reunion," Michelle said, succumbing to another happy giggle.

Kate slid her gaze from Michelle to me and back again. "You knew?"

Michelle's smile softened. "Price called me last week. All he said was to book this place for the two of us and to keep it a secret. That's why everything came together so quickly. I had to get you here as soon as possible."

Kate shook her head again, fresh tears rimming her eyes and catching on her long lashes.

"Sweetheart..." I took a step toward her.

"Don't sweetheart me!" She slammed her hand against the marble. "You were dead. We buried you!"

Michelle set the champagne bottle down. "You deserve some space. I'm sorry," she said gently. "I'm going to go explore the island a little. I'll be back before dark." Looking down, she brushed past me, but not before pressing another quick kiss to my cheek.

Then she disappeared, leaving me alone with my wife. My very angry, passionate, beautiful wife. The woman I could make come in under a minute. The woman I'd vowed to love my entire life.

The woman who'd endured my funeral...

My jaw tensed almost painfully with that vision. Kate, shrouded in black, saying goodbye to me forever among our family and friends.

"There was nothing in that casket, Kate."

If they'd found a body, I wouldn't be standing here right now.

Her head fell into her hands and she sobbed quietly. I resisted the urge to take her into my arms again.

"I know you're upset—"

She shot her head up and narrowed her eyes. "Upset? You left me alone, Price. For a year, you left me to pick up the pieces of our life. Where were you while my heart was rotting? Island hopping? Surfing?"

She gestured up and down the length of my tanned and toned body as if I'd scrubbed all signs of life from my identity to go on an extended vacation. She was dead wrong.

I closed the space between us, bringing her hard against me. I wasn't letting her go this time. "I did this for us! I did this for you, Kate. You don't understand right now, but trust me. There was no other way."

She swallowed, her anger and her tears seeming to subside for the moment.

"I love you," I said between gritted teeth. God help me, she'd never know how much. "I'm alive, but part of me died when that plane went down. I want it back. I want *you* back."

She tried shaking her head again, but I caught her cheek and tilted her face up, stilling her. Our lips were so close. If only I could make her understand everything with a kiss, a promise that my heart had been in the right place this whole time.

It was worth a try. So I took her mouth, delving past her lips until I found her velvet tongue. Then I took more. I should have celebrated the soft wonder of her lips against mine, but instead I consumed. I devoured her until we could scarcely breathe. When we finally broke apart, I was panting and desperately hard, equal parts heartbroken and restored, conflicted and at peace now that she was close enough to hold.

"Kate, I have to be with you." My voice cracked with barely harnessed need.

She lifted on her toes, sifting her fingers through my overgrown hair as she brought our lips together again. Like an ice cube in the summer sun, something melted inside me—the fear and doubt that had taken hold the second she'd recoiled from my touch. No. She was still my Kate. And I'd show her I was still the man I once was, in all the ways that mattered.

I lifted her against me, hooking her thighs over my hips as I journeyed out of the main living area into the nearest bedroom. I kicked the door shut with my heel and lowered Kate to her feet by the bed. Her eyes were hazy with lust. In that moment, I vowed to keep that look on her face as often as I could for as long as she was here.

I trailed my hands over her shoulders and down her arms. I was going to make love to her. Then I was going to feed her. And then... At some point, I'd have to give her some answers. But first she'd have to make a choice. One that would make or break our future. As much as I loved her, the choice had to be hers.

Before I could dwell on that, she reached for me, sliding my white linen shirt over my shoulders. Then she tugged at the drawstring of my shorts. "Take these off."

Her tone wasn't teasing or playful. It almost bordered on desperate. I knew because I was nothing short of possessed by the thought of having her naked, bared and open to me as I drove our bodies together until she cried out. I flinched when her touch grazed my cock, which was hard as fucking granite already.

Quickly I shucked the shorts. Her half-lidded eyes flicked wider, but I couldn't torture myself with her hot stare on me a minute more. I tugged at the knot that held her sarong in place and pulled the ties of her bikini until it lay on the floor.

Pushing her back onto the bed, I followed, kneeing her legs apart so I could take the space between them. Everything inside me wanted to take her right then, but I worried she was too fragile. The last thing I wanted was to hurt her, or scare her with the beast inside me that hadn't been fed in a year. The beast that only hungered for one woman. Only her body called to me, her scent, the taste of her perfect pussy.

The thought occurred to me then that she could have been with other people. Who knew what temptations she'd faced in her grief, believing I was gone forever? I pushed the thought quickly away. I'd forgive her, because I was the one who needed real forgiving for the hell I'd put her through.

With a groan I crawled lower, diving into the sweet heaven between her thighs. I breathed curses against her wet flesh, plunging my fingers into her, testing her, remembering her...

"I still feel like I must be dreaming. This can't really be happening," she said breathily, sliding her fingers through my hair.

Fucking hell, I wasn't an apparition. I was her husband. I moved up her body. Sealing our mouths together with a hot kiss, I pressed the head of my cock against her opening.

"You're not dreaming. I'm real. This..." I pushed into her, as deeply as I could go. "This is real."

She arched her back and gasped against my lips. My God, she was beautiful. A dozen buried memories came to the surface in that moment. The first time I'd had her. The last time. Times when I'd made her say crazy dirty things in the heat of the moment. When I'd made even dirtier promises and delivered on them.

I brushed my lips along the column of her neck. "And when I make you come, Kate, you'll know it's real. No dream can do what I'm about to do to you."

I pulled out only to slide in again, slowly this time, savoring every inch of the journey of our two bodies becoming one. She released a small cry and dug her nails into my shoulder. Fuck, I'd missed that sound. Birds, waves crashing against the rocks, orchestras. The rest of the world could have it. The only sound I wanted in my ears was the music of my wife's delirious cries while I fucked her dizzy.

"Does it feel real now, sweetheart?" I punctuated it with a hard shove that brought our hips tightly together.

"Yes...yes."

The word pushed past her lips a few more times to the rhythm of my thrusts.

I could spend forever this way.

I would. *We* would...

I kissed her again, slowly and deeply, wishing I could suspend time and stay in this moment forever. We deserved hours of fucking and multiple twenty-minute orgasms after what we'd been through. But I hadn't prepared myself for how intense sex would be after a year without. And suddenly all I cared about was getting her there before I did.

I slipped out of her and yanked her down the bed until her ass rested on the edge. I kissed her smooth calves as I positioned them atop my shoulders.

She trailed her fingertips down my abdomen, a motion that pushed her breasts together in a most lovely way. "But I want to touch you."

I slipped my cock back into her wet heat, holding back a groan from the incredible sensation. "You can. Right after you come, baby. I'm not going to last long."

With that, I started pumping in earnest, keeping her hips at the perfect angle to hit her G-spot and send her into orbit. A decade could go by, and I'd still know the combination to this lock.

Her moans grew louder, and as soon as I started thumbing her clit, everything tensed up. Her fists balled, her toes pointed, and my balls drew up. So close. So fucking close.

"I love you, Kate...so much. Oh, fuck..."

She screamed. I might have blacked out. I lost track of her orgasm as mine barreled through me, rocking me as I rocked into her with the last drive of my hips.

I slipped out and joined her on the bed before my legs gave out. Tucking Kate beside me, I felt more content than I could ever remember.

Beside us stood a wall of windows overlooking the ocean and open sliding doors that led to another private lanai. A warm breeze blew gently through the room, billowing the silky curtains around the bed. I released a sigh made of pure bliss.

If I was dead, this was heaven.

Then Kate perched on her elbow and looked down on me like a blue-eyed angel. I reached up and touched her face, mesmerized by her softness. I traced every line and reintroduced myself to the faint freckles that crept up on the apples of her cheeks when they saw the sunshine.

She'll say yes. She has to.

In that moment, I believed it. Then she finally spoke.

"You have to tell me everything."

CHAPTER THREE

Kate

He didn't respond right away, and though I was desperate for answers, I didn't press him. Right now, I had to touch him. I wanted—no, *needed*—to have our skin in contact. Without contact, he might disappear in a flash, and I'd wake up, only to have been caught up in a dream.

I'd had similar dreams during the past year, some so real I'd awoken smiling and warm with afterglow, only for tears to choke me when I realized Price was gone and I was in bed alone.

His shoulders were still broad and strong, more bronze than I remembered, no doubt from the tropical sunshine. His dark hair had grown longer and now covered his ears, but it still felt like fine silk between my fingers. His finely muscled chest and abdomen still stole my breath, and when I trailed my fingers over one nipple, he inhaled and closed his eyes, just like he always had. Still so responsive to my every touch.

His lips were full and pink, and a few days' growth of beard laced his jawline. This was different. Price had always been clean-shaven. I cupped his cheek, letting the onyx stubble scrape against my fingertips. Yes, different. Different but good. He looked rugged. Gorgeous and rugged.

And then I looked into his warm brown eyes, and a chill speared through me. His eyes had changed. He still looked at me with the same intensity, the same love, but something new gazed out at me as well.

Those eyes had seen things. They shone with a new understanding, a dark understanding that had been forced upon him.

Price might look basically the same, might still love me and be able to bring me quivering to my knees, but something had changed within him.

"Price," I said again, "you have to tell me everything."

He sighed, nodding. "You deserve as much, but you have to understand. I can't tell you everything. Not yet. Not if I'm going to keep you safe."

Chills gripped the back of my neck. Keep me safe? For the first time, reality hit me like a cement block. Price hadn't died in that commuter plane crash. Price had lived, had *chosen* not to come back to me. He'd faked his death.

A man didn't fake his own death for the fun of it. That haunted understanding I saw in Price's eyes? It had led him here. Led *us* here. But whatever the reason, had it been enough to keep us apart for a year?

Every cell in my body screamed at me to pull him to me, to kiss him, to forget the last year. What did any of it matter? Price was back. Literally back from the dead. We could have those babies now. We could grow old together. We had a second chance—

No. I shook my head, still cupping his cheek. I couldn't let go of him. Couldn't risk him disappearing in a puff of smoke. "You owe me the whole story. You disappeared." Sobs choked me. "You let me think you were dead!"

He swallowed, his Adam's apple bobbing in his neck. "I've thought of you every day. Every fucking minute of every fucking day."

"Do you think I haven't thought of you? You were my life, Price. And you let me mourn you, bury you. How can I get past that?"

"I know this is difficult to understand, but there were circumstances—"

"Circumstances you won't let me in on. At least you knew I was alive! You weren't plagued with visions of my body plummeting to the ground, erupting in flames."

"God, baby." He closed his eyes, wincing. "Please. Don't do this."

"*You* did this, Price. You chose this. You chose not to come back to me. I was a good wife, damn it! Why did you do this?"

"Kate, please." He grabbed my wrist and removed my hand from his face. He pressed a soft kiss to my palm. "I will tell you everything when I can. There will be time. I promise. For now, can't we just enjoy our reunion? Embrace this night?"

I let out a soft huff. "Is this the only night we'll have?"

This time he cupped my cheek, and his dark eyes smoked with intensity. "That's up to you."

Up to me? "What the—"

His lips came down on mine, not softly this time. This time he took, and I let him, opening for him as if by instinct. My mouth, my body responded to his, just as it always had. Just as it always would.

Our kisses had always been passionate, always flaming hot, but this one blazed through me like wildfire. Our tongues tangled and dueled until Price finally broke away, panting.

"You're mine, Kate. You'll always be mine." He crushed his mouth to my lips again.

I hadn't been his for the past year... But my thoughts stopped there as his kiss overpowered me again. My nipples hardened and poked into his smooth chest, aching for his touch, his lips. When they could no longer stand being ignored, I broke the kiss.

"Price. My nipples. *Please*."

He cupped my breasts. "So beautiful." He stroked the tops of my breasts, avoiding my wrinkled areolas and aching peaks.

"Please!"

He smiled and took a nipple between his full lips. The surge arrowed straight into my pussy. I loved having my nipples sucked, and no one sucked them like Price.

"Mine," he said against my flesh. "All mine."

I moaned as he twisted the other nipple between his thumb and forefinger. Sparks radiated through me, culminating in the ache between my legs. Price continued sucking while he trailed his free hand over my abdomen, leaving electricity in his wake. When he found my clit, I arched into his fingers.

He let my nipple drop from his lips. "God, you're dripping wet, Kate." He smoothed his fingers over my slick folds and then slid down my body, the heat of his muscled flesh scorching me. "Too long since I've tasted this sweetness. Too fucking long."

My eyes were closed when he swiped his tongue across my slit, but then I opened them, and sure enough, he was there, gazing into my eyes like he always had, his own dark and full of desire.

I stared into his eyes, and then I saw his soul. He was there. The same Price. Things might have changed in the last year, but he was still Price. And he was still mine.

He tugged and sucked, murmuring against my inner thighs, growling as he ate me. I climbed higher and higher, and when I was near the peak—could actually see the snow-capped Adirondacks in my mind's eye—he thrust two fingers into me and I flew.

"God, Price!" My body quivered around me, my blood whooshing like boiled honey through my veins.

"That's it, sweetness. Come. Come for me. Only for me."

He continued pushing his fingers into me, caressing my G-spot, and as my convulsions were settling, I took wing once more, this time my womb pulsing deeply, the kind of climax that sank inward toward my heart, toward my soul.

Before I could open my mouth and beg him to get inside me, Price was hovering over me, his cock head tickling my clit.

"God, please," I gasped.

He plunged into me, touching my innermost secret place, uniting not only our bodies but our spirits. It was earthy. It was passionate. It was the most basic life force.

It was love.

I gave in to the moment, to the pleasure he evoked in me. All thoughts fled from my mind, leaving only feeling. Pure emotion. It coursed through me like a warm summer breeze, taking me with it and leaving the past year in the dust.

Only now mattered. Only this moment. This man.

He fucked me hard, tiny drops of perspiration emerging on his brow, and never once did he move his gaze from mine.

"This is us, baby. This is real. This is what we can have. Forever." He thrust harder, his pubic bone pummeling into my clit and making my skin prickle. Soon I was on the verge of another climax, my whole body singing like a choral symphony.

"I'm going to come, Kate. I'm going to come. Come with me, sweetness. Now."

His words tipped me over the edge, and I sprang forward, giving him everything I had. Everything I was.

"I love you, Kate," he said, wincing as he released into me.

"I love you too. Always."

♦ ♦ ♦ ♦

I opened my eyes. I was still in the downstairs bedroom, the one Michelle had chosen for herself, my body tangled in the soft cotton sheet. I sat up, blinking. Darkness had descended.

Price. Where was Price?

No. It hadn't all been a dream.

My pulse racing, I got up, wrapped my sarong around me in a makeshift sundress, checked myself in the bathroom mirror, and left the bedroom. I found Price and Michelle on the front lanai. I opened the door.

Michelle stopped speaking abruptly before I could catch what she'd been saying. "Kate. Come join us."

Price stood. "Hey, you. Did you have a good nap?"

In truth, I'd slept better for those few hours than I had in the last year. But I said only, "Yes."

I took the seat Price was holding out for me, and Michelle started pouring me a glass of wine, but I shook my head. I didn't want to drink right now. I looked to my husband, and in the moonlight, the haunted understanding in his eyes was even more apparent. What had he and Michelle been talking about?

I inhaled and let out a slow breath. "Go ahead and talk about whatever you were talking about."

"We were just making small talk." Michelle took a sip of her wine, not meeting my gaze.

"Yeah? Small talk about what?"

"Nothing, baby," Price said. "Chelle was just filling me in on Mom and Dad."

"Yeah, and they're both going to kick your ass if they ever find out what you're up to," she said.

Price laughed—a strange sound that wasn't like his normal laugh. But what did I know about what was normal anymore? Price had touched my soul earlier both times we made love, and for a few blissful, sacred moments, reality had been suspended.

Reality was back now. With a vengeance.

Price, still standing, turned to Michelle. "Would you mind excusing us? I'd like to take my wife on a walk."

Michelle smiled. "Of course not. Please. Go."

He turned to me then. "Kate?"

I sighed and stood. So there would be a walk. But would there be a talk? Or would we end up making love under the stars? I couldn't help how my body responded to Price, but at some point, I was going to require some answers.

He looked amazing, his dark hair in disarray, his white linen shirt covering his chest. A few buttons were undone, his bronze beauty teasing me. Even his feet were gorgeous in his Tevas. His well-formed legs, corded with muscle, were flexed and ready to walk. Or maybe run.

He was tense. I'd known him long enough to read him like a book.

I stood and put my hand in his.

"I'm going to whip up something for a late dinner," Michelle said. "I made sure the kitchen was stocked. Be back in about an hour if you want some."

"Okay. Thanks, Sis." Price led me off of the lanai and onto the light sand.

I squished my toes into the warmth. "I forgot my flip-flops."

"No worries. If I see a jelly fish, I'll carry you." He smiled.

"I was thinking more of stepping on sharp shells," I said. "I'll be back in a minute." I headed inside.

Michelle was already pulling veggies out of the crisper. "Did you decide not to go?"

"No. Just getting my shoes." I headed into the downstairs bedroom and retrieved them.

"How about shrimp stir-fry?" Michelle said when I walked by the kitchen.

"Sure. Great." All food had tasted like dirt for the past year, so what did I care? Maybe tonight I'd actually experience flavor again.

"Hey...Kate?"

I turned back toward the kitchen. "Yeah?"

"Go easy on him. He's been through...a lot."

"I get that, Chelle. I really do. I don't know what happened yet, but it can't be pretty." I sighed. "I've been through a lot too. And not just me. You, Brenda and Sonny, all of his extended family and friends..." I shook my head. "He won't tell me anything."

"I know. I'm sorry." She looked down at the cutting board she'd pulled out of a cupboard.

Her reaction niggled at the back of my neck. "Wait. Has he told you anything?" A spear of envy lanced through me.

"No. Not really."

"What the hell does that mean?"

"Nothing. It means nothing."

Michelle and I had been friends since she was a freshman and I was a junior in college. We'd met through Price, of course, but we'd become close independent of him. I trusted her, but right now, she wasn't telling me something.

"It has to come from Price," she said. "Now go on. Make up for lost time. You both deserve that."

I nodded and headed onto the lanai. Price stayed silent when he took my hand. We walked away from the villa, the light of the moon casting a silver glow over us.

After we'd walked for several minutes, Price looked up. "The stars are amazing here. No pollution and smog to hide them."

I looked at the sky. The stars did indeed seem more sparkling and numerous. "They're dazzling," I said.

"Not as dazzling as you are." He cupped my cheeks and gave me a chaste kiss on my lips. "Can you ever forgive me, Kate?"

What a loaded question. Price was the love of my life. There was a time when I'd never imagined he could do anything that would require my forgiveness. Perhaps he still hadn't.

"You said something earlier. You said whether we had more than one night was up to me."

"Yes."

"What does that mean?"

He brushed his hand from my cheek, over my shoulder, and down my arm, making it tingle. "It means I can never go back, Kate."

"Why?"

"Because I know things. Things I shouldn't know."

"Tell me. Tell me what you know." I stroked his strong forearm, an overwhelming urge to love him and protect him billowing through me. "Maybe we can fix it. We always said we could get through anything together."

He closed his eyes, sighed, and then opened them and looked again to the stars. "God, you're so innocent. So was I until about a year and a half ago."

My arms caught a chill, and I rubbed them despite the warm night air. "Price, you're scaring me."

"I don't mean to, baby. I don't want to. Maybe I'm being selfish, dragging you and my sister into this. Maybe I should have left well enough alone, let you get on with your life."

"Price, please."

He brushed his hands over my shoulders and down my arms, taking both of my hands. "That commuter plane going down was supposed to kill me, and thank God they thought it had. Otherwise, I really would be dead right now. So would my parents. So would Chelle." He closed his eyes, grimacing. "And so would you."

CHAPTER FOUR

Price

The truth was sharp and painful, like a herd of angry bulls tearing through me, demanding to be set free. The truth could get us all killed. But any illusions I'd had about keeping Kate and Chelle in the dark about what really happened to me were chipping away as the hours passed.

I parted my lips, expecting the words to spill free. But when I opened my eyes, Kate's beauty stole the moment. No one and nothing had ever been more precious to me. Anything would be worth keeping her safe. I'd die for her, and I would do it all over again if it meant she kept breathing. As desperate as I was to be with her now, I couldn't forget how perilous things could become again.

I squeezed Kate's hands in mine. "My coming back into your life puts everyone at risk again. I need you to understand that."

She nodded slightly.

"Every day I wanted to reach out to you. Every day I didn't meant the people who wanted me dead could believe I really was."

Tears glistened in her eyes, sparkling like the moonlight on the waves crashing softly against the shore. "What kind of person could ever want you dead?"

If she only knew. One person with deadly intent I could have handled. I could have maneuvered and gotten our lives back on track. But greed with roots wide and deep had paid for my plane to go down. That wasn't vengeance. That was a war I couldn't possibly win.

"It doesn't matter, baby. What matters is that if they knew I was alive and breathing right now, they'd want to do something about it. They can't ever find out."

"But Chelle mentioned your parents. Aren't you going to tell them you're alive? I thought we were going home after all this."

I shook my head, hoping the reality of what I was proposing wasn't more painful than what she'd already lived through. "Chelle promised me she wouldn't say anything yet. What she doesn't know is that they have to keep believing I'm gone, at least for now."

"What about us?"

I swallowed hard because I had a feeling the next few minutes would change our future forever. I'd just gotten her back. That quickly, I could lose her again.

"I told you we have tonight, Kate. We have the rest of this trip together if you want it. After that...you can either go back home without me—"

"No!" She fisted her hands in my shirt and closed the distance between us. A tear journeyed slowly down her cheek as she gazed up at me, the anguish of that possibility plain in her eyes. "You can't ask me to do that, Price. Not now, after everything we've been through."

I wiped away her tear and cradled her face in my palms. "I'm not. I'm asking you to come *with me* instead."

The ocean breeze whistled through the palm trees, rustling over the silence that stretched between us.

"I don't understand. This isn't making sense. I love you. I want our life back." Her voice trembled.

I wanted to kiss her again. Communicate everything I couldn't tell her with the press of our lips together, the perfect harmony of our flesh when it met and joined.

"Kate, we would have to disappear...forever. Start a new life."

She shook her head and took a small step away from me. "There has to be another way."

"I wish there were."

Even as I said the words, I questioned how I could ask her to make such a sacrifice. For me. For us. For the love that still burned so brightly between us. I was asking her to give up her life for the only one we could have together.

An unspoken answer lingered behind her beautiful eyes, twisting my heart into a desperate bloodless organ in my chest. The rejection I feared would come next roiled deeply within me, spurring me to speak my next words quickly.

"You don't have to decide right now. I know what I'm asking you to give up, because I had to give it up too. Except I never had a choice."

"You *had* a choice."

Resentment and pain laced her words, and I felt like we were right back where we started on the beach a few hours ago. Would she never understand how painful it had been for me to walk away from our life together?

"Protecting you was never a choice. It's the way it has to be." I came to her, brought her against my chest, and hugged her tightly. "I know not everything makes sense. You have questions that I might never be able to answer. But if you decide to go back home, it's better this way. Trust me."

I expected her to throw some more anger at me, but after a short intake of breath, she began sobbing quietly in my arms.

I wasn't sure which felt worse—her verbal lashings or her tears. Both cut me to the bone.

Our reunion thus far had been the ultimate emotional roller coaster. When she wasn't crying, she was screaming out in ecstasy from my tongue or my cock. I could bring her so high and so low. Both came too easily. Could we have a future made of pleasure, or was I damning her to a life of regret for all that she would leave behind?

I kissed the top of her head and hushed her. All I could do was show her my love and let her decide. Whatever path she chose would be the right one. I had to believe it.

"Price?"

My stomach clenched at the sound of her watery voice as I anticipated an answer I wasn't ready to hear yet. "What is it, sweetheart?"

"I love you."

I squeezed my eyes closed and released a heavy sigh. "I love you too."

We stood that way a long time, holding each other, swaying together as night fell around us. Why did every moment with her feel so timeless? Nothing could be more cruel when time was anything but on my side.

"Come on," I finally said. "Let's go eat."

◆ ◆ ◆ ◆

Chelle moved around the kitchen and set the table for dinner with the same bubbly energy I remembered her always having. But as she sat to join Kate and me at the table, her bright smile seemed too wide, almost forced. Perhaps she was doing it for Kate's benefit. She'd made no secret of Kate's depressed state following my supposed death, another unfortunate circumstance heaved onto the pile of my regrets of leaving her. I imagined Chelle had played a big part in keeping my wife's spirits above water over this past year, and for that I would always be grateful.

I glanced back to Kate, who was staring blankly at her water glass. I took a generous gulp of wine, pushing down the guilt, and reached for something lighter.

"How are things going at the *Tribune*?"

Kate lifted her gaze to mine and blinked a few times, as if she'd been somewhere far away. "Um...slow, I guess."

"Why?"

She shrugged and scooped some stir-fry onto her plate. "I stepped away from the staff position for a while. The schedule was too much for me...with everything else that was going on."

I frowned. When I'd decided to go off the grid, I'd known that she'd be set financially for several years. Along with the substantial life insurance she'd collected on, I'd been pulling down seven-figures as a day trader, leaving her with a healthy savings account. What concerned me more than her stepping away from the job was that someone as brilliant as Kate would let her career stagnate.

"Are you still writing?" I asked.

"She did a great freelance piece on the tourism protests in Spain earlier this year," Chelle piped in. "You should do more things like that. You were so rejuvenated after that trip."

Kate lifted an eyebrow, her expression the perfect non-verbal retort to Chelle's unfailing positivity. I had to laugh out loud. Kate's facial expressions were a language all their own, and over the years we'd spent together, I'd become fluent. I knew when I was in deep shit with her before she could say a word.

She slid her gaze to mine and lifted the corners of her lips into a knowing smirk. "It was a good trip. All things considered."

Chelle slapped her arm. "I saw you smile more than I had in months afterward. Maybe you and Price can take a trip there after you get settled back home."

Kate smiled, but it never reached her eyes. "Maybe."

I downed the last of my wine and poured another glass. I had to stop reading into every word and every look, hoping to find her answer there. Damn it, maybe I should have told her that she *couldn't* give me an answer until the end of the trip. Then I wouldn't live in fear of the word "no" flying past her lips and destroying every chance I had for happiness in this life.

"What do you lovebirds plan to do tomorrow? Are you staying in or...?" Chelle winked.

I laughed again. Sister or not, she surely couldn't ignore that my reunion with Kate would involve sex. Lots of it, if I had any choice in the matter. I was content spending the next few weeks exclusively between the sheets with my wife, but something told me that wouldn't be enough to convince her to spend the rest of her life with me again.

"I was thinking about giving Kate a tour of the boat tomorrow, actually. It's nothing special, but it's home. We can cruise around some of the little islands around Leiloa."

New warmth glittered in the cool blue of Kate's eyes, releasing some tension I'd been holding.

"I'd like that," she said with a small smile.

Mercifully, we spent the rest of the dinner listening to Chelle update me about her life in the city, from bad dates to a well-deserved promotion. I was grateful for the moment to ignore the minefield of Kate's and my past. I'd done enough traversing of it today and had survived relatively unscathed.

The three of us laughed, finished the bottle of wine, and I caught Kate plating up seconds of the stir-fry, which satisfied me. Gradually, relief settled over my earlier anxiety. Kate moved her bags to the downstairs bedroom while I helped Chelle clean up the dishes from dinner.

"How was the walk?" Chelle asked in a hushed tone.

I shrugged, because no answer was simple. "It went okay. Are you all right with the plan tomorrow? I didn't mean to leave you out. Kate and I... We just have a lot to work through, you know?"

Chelle canted her head and glanced up at me from under her dark lashes. "Price, I love you, but I'm not here to be a third wheel while you two rediscover each other. It's been a year. Honestly, I can't imagine what you're both going through right now, but I'm sure it can't be easy. Suffice to say, I'm just happy you're alive. We'll catch up once things are right with you and Kate."

My throat tightened, but I masked anything else in my

expression that would give away the fact that after this trip, I'd be absent from my family's life again. I could only handle so much heartbreak in one day. I could only hope she'd forgive me eventually.

After we said good night, I went to find Kate, who'd been quiet since we finished dinner. The light was on in the bedroom, illuminating her still figure on the unmade bed. She lay on her side, her arms tucked close to her chest, her sarong fanned out in colorful waves on the sheets. I stood at the foot of the bed and watched her shallow breathing, her peaceful countenance.

My angel. My life.

I didn't know how many minutes passed that way. But being able to treasure her on this side of her dreams was a perfect way to end a day that had been fraught with emotional pitfalls.

I undressed, turned out the light, and nestled beside her. She sighed when I brought her warm body against mine. I could have undressed her. We'd always slept naked together. But the hint of her curves molding to me through the thin fabric already had the blood rushing to my cock. I'd never stop wanting her, never stop worshiping the way she seemed made for me and only me. But tonight I had to let her rest.

Tonight she'd sleep in my arms, and we'd face whatever tomorrow brought together.

CHAPTER FIVE

Kate

I awoke to the first rays of sunlight streaming through the window. For a moment, I panicked. I was back in our brownstone, waking up alone to another day without the love of my life.

But there he was, beside me, the covers tangled around his waist, just as they always had since the first time we'd shared a night together. My sarong had loosened during the night, and I lay naked next to my husband.

Déjà vu.

A very welcome déjà vu.

Price's breathing was steady and shallow, just as I remembered. His dark hair, tousled and sexy, was a gorgeous contrast against the stark whiteness of the pillow on which he rested his head. His full lips were parted slightly as he exhaled puffs of air.

How had I existed this past year without him? I couldn't help a quiet but sarcastic chuckle. Existing. That's what I'd been doing. Simply existing. While I'd enjoyed the trip to Spain and had smiled a few times, I still hadn't been living.

If I chose to stay here, to give up everything else in my life—my home, my family, my friends, my work—I could stop merely existing. With Price, I would *live*.

Yet how could I leave everything behind? To never see my mother, father, brother, and sister again, never know my nieces and nephews. And what of them? Would they think me dead? Kidnapped? What would I be allowed to tell them?

What about children? God, children... My own children would never know their grandparents, their aunts and uncles, their cousins. Was that fair? Would we always be looking over our shoulders for the next potential threat? I'd dreamed of having Price's children from the first moment I'd laid eyes on his dark beauty, but would that be possible now? I couldn't bear the thought of putting a child in danger. Would I be giving up my dream to be a mother?

I'd be giving up everything.

Everything except Price.

Looking over at him, the sun illuminating his bronze chest, I thought for a moment I could do it, that it would be worth it. After all, Price was the love of my life. He was more important than everyone and everything else in my life combined.

That didn't lessen the importance of those others, though, and the impact my disappearing would have on them.

But how I loved this man. My Price. It was the kind of love that filled my heart, my soul—the kind of love that almost hurt in its intensity. A good hurt, though. A fulfilling hurt.

A year had passed, and still I loved him. I hadn't even begun to get over him, and here he was, alive, and opening up a second chance for the two of us.

I didn't need to decide right now. At this moment, I would

savor him. Just staring at his god-like exquisiteness filled me with immeasurable joy. That face, that body—I'd never imagined I would look upon them again. Touch them again.

I feathered my fingertips over his solid shoulder. He shuddered slightly but didn't awaken. I smiled. His sheer masculine beauty would always rob me of breath. I trailed my hand over his chest to his waist, untangling the sheet and baring the rest of him to me. His well-formed legs, the black curls between them...and his gorgeous cock, now flaccid.

I could take care of that.

I lowered my head, inhaled his musky maleness, and then pressed tiny kisses onto him.

He responded instantly, hardening to my touch. I swirled my tongue around him, tracing the purple vein that marbled around his shaft, just as I remembered. Still so velvety smooth under my tongue, still warm with a pleasant zing of saltiness.

Déjà vu.

I looked up.

His eyes were open now...and full of fire. "God. Don't stop, baby."

I had no intention of stopping. I licked along the tip and then sucked the bulbous head into my mouth, pulling. He groaned. I slid my lips along the length of him until he nudged the back of my throat. I eased up and then took him in again.

And again he groaned.

I'd been a novice at giving head when Price and I had started dating, but he'd been a patient teacher. Now I loved it, loved the power it gave me to bring him to his knees. This was so personal to me, so intimate. After Price died, I'd wondered if I'd ever be able to put another man's cock into my mouth.

Now I knew the truth. Never. I could only do this for Price.

I added my hand to the motion, twisting my fist as I slid my lips up and down his cock, adding suction and then releasing it, my pussy growing wet as I brought my husband to the edge.

"Kate, baby..." His voice was low. "Stop. I want to be inside you."

I closed my eyes. I ached for that too—that glorious fullness that only Price could provide. But at this moment, I needed something else. This power. I'd been so helpless for the last year, so chained up by a string of events over which I had no control.

Right now I had control, and I wasn't giving it up.

I dropped his cock from my mouth, still grasping it, and met his dark gaze. "Later. Right now I need you. I need you to come in my mouth."

"But baby—"

I silenced him as I glided my lips to his base again.

"Ah, God," he groaned, closing his eyes. "I've missed you so much, Kate. So fucking much. No one else could ever make me feel the way you do."

I worked him with my hand as I licked his balls, kissed his inner thighs, all the while reveling in his deep groans, his words of praise.

When his balls and cock tightened, and I knew he was ready, I plunged my mouth onto his cock and took all of him. As his essence torched the back of my throat, I moaned my satisfaction.

I released him, raining tiny kisses over his cock and thighs and then climbing up and nestling myself in the crook of his arm. "I love you, Price."

"God, Kate, I love you so much."

I closed my eyes. I was turned on, ready to go. I knew I could get Price to give me an orgasm without much urging, but I didn't move. I wasn't yet ready to give up my power, to become slave to circumstances and situations beyond my control once more. Instead, I breathed in deeply, and for a timeless moment, I imagined we could stay like this forever, in this magical place, without any consequences.

I immersed myself in that dream until I drifted back to sleep.

◆ ◆ ◆ ◆

"Mmm..."

Price was licking my nipples. I'd thought I was dreaming, but this was reality. He moved down my body and spread my legs.

I smiled and opened my eyes.

He was gazing at me. "Thought I'd return the favor." He swiped his tongue over my wet folds.

"How long was I asleep?" I asked.

"Who knows?" He kissed my pussy. "Who cares?"

Who cared indeed? Why not continue my dream for a bit? *Price and I together forever. No consequences...*

"You taste so sweet, Kate." He burrowed into me.

I lifted my hips, giving him better access, letting his tongue reach my innermost places. I chilled all over, my pussy throbbing, while he tormented me as only he could. In less than a minute I was close to the peak.

"There you go, sweetness. There you go." He slid two fingers into me.

I unraveled, my whole body flashing with shards of electricity. He knew exactly what to do, exactly what buttons to push to bring me to ecstasy.

"You're so beautiful when you come, Kate. Your body flushes a rosy pink, and those noises you make... God." He continued to finger me, brushing up against my G-spot. "I swear I could be happy just making you come. Just tasting this heaven between your legs." He touched his tongue to my clit once more.

I soared again, this time higher, screaming his name as stars burst through my body. He was my world, this man. He was my reason for living. I closed my eyes and then squealed as he filled me with his hard cock. His lips met mine, our tongues dancing.

This was the true power. The two of us together. There was power in this kind of love.

He broke the kiss. "Kate, baby..." He breathed rapidly and increased the speed of his thrusts. "Can't"—*thrust*—"live"—*thrust*—"without you." *Thrust.* "God, yes."

He released into me, clamping his lips onto mine and kissing me deeply. We stayed joined for several minutes, kissing, and then just holding each other.

Again I imagined staying here forever. No consequences.

But morning had come, and with it, consequences.

When Price rolled off of me onto his side, I turned to face him. "Price."

"Hmm?" His eyes were closed.

"What about your parents? My parents? My brother and sister? I have nieces and nephews, Price. I have—"

He opened his eyes and touched his fingers to my lips. "Baby."

I shook my head. "What about children? We always wanted children. Would they be safe?"

He sighed. "I...don't know, Kate."

"Then how can you—"

He placed his fingers on my lips again. "We'll talk about all of that. We'll talk about everything. We'll figure it all out. I promise. But can we just have today? I want to show you my boat. I want to show you the rest of this amazing island. I want to hold your hand, walk with you, smile, laugh, just *be*."

"I'd love that. Really. But we can't escape reality, Price. You know that as well as I do. What you're asking me to do has repercussions."

He sighed again and sat up. "Breakfast?"

"You're changing the subject."

He smiled, leaned down, and brushed his lips across mine. "Damn right."

I couldn't help returning his smile. "We have to consider these things at some point. And even more importantly, you need to tell me the whole truth."

He cupped my cheek, his dark eyes heavy-lidded. "Kate, please. Just today. Give me today. Let me show you what kind of life I can give you here."

He didn't look sad, exactly. I could usually read Price well, but right now his feelings eluded me. His hand still rested on my face, and I placed mine over it.

"I would do anything for you. I can give you today."

"Thank you." He rose from the bed and put on the pair of shorts he'd worn yesterday. "Let's get a cup of coffee, okay? I need to let Chelle know what we'll be up to. Then we can shower and get moving."

I nodded, got up, and wrapped my sarong around me. We headed downstairs to the kitchen.

Michelle was sitting at the table, a half-eaten plate of fruit in front of her. "I was beginning to give up on you two." She winked.

I'd long since gotten over being embarrassed around Michelle. She knew I thought her brother was the sexiest man on the planet. I opened my mouth to speak, but she stopped me with a gesture.

"Please, spare me the gory details. I know you're head over heels in love with the man of your dreams, but he's still my big brother."

I smiled, poured two cups of coffee, and handed one to Price.

"Fruit in the fridge," Michelle said. "There's also bacon, eggs, some wholegrain bread, and yogurt."

"Fruit's fine for me." I opened the refrigerator and grabbed containers of cut-up pineapple and mango. Price would never go for fruit, though.

"Which one of you women wants to make me a hearty omelet?" Price turned the corners of his lips up into a devilish smile.

Michelle rolled her eyes. "I don't do breakfast food. Besides, I made dinner last night."

Price loved eggs. I'd made him many omelets in the past simply because he loved them. My first attempts had been scrambled eggs speckled with peppers, onions, and colored orange from cheddar cheese, but I'd gotten better over the years. I didn't like eggs much myself, and I wasn't a great cook, but I loved making omelets for Price.

"I'll do it, babe," I said.

He kissed my cheek. "I've had to make my own omelets for the past year. They don't hold a candle to yours, Kate."

My omelets were hardly legendary, but I understood what he wasn't saying. He loved my omelets because I made them, just as I loved making them because I was making them for him.

My eyes filled, and suddenly the dam broke and sobs began to rack my body.

Price came to me swiftly and wrapped me in his strong arms. "What is it, baby?"

I hiccupped. "It's nothing. It's just...the omelet."

"You don't have to make an omelet. It's okay."

"No." I rubbed my nose on his bare shoulder. "That's not it. I want to make it. I just... I never thought I'd make you an omelet again."

"Shh," he said. "I promise. You can make as many omelets as you want."

I choked out a laugh at the absurdity of crying like a fool over eggs I'd never liked making in the first place and then turned around toward the table. "Michelle?"

"I think she discreetly disappeared when the waterworks started."

I sighed. "I'm sorry."

"Hey"—Price stroked my cheek, brushing away tears—"you don't ever have to be sorry about anything. You hear me? This is all on me. All me."

I buried my face in his hard chest, my nose still running. Price thought he was speaking the truth when he said this was all on him, but he wasn't. I was involved now. Any decision I made had consequences for both of us and for myriad others.

This was on *us* now.

But I'd promised him today—today free of concerns and worry over fallout. I'd never yet broken a promise to my husband, and I wouldn't start now. I gulped down my last sob and pulled away, grabbing a tissue from the counter. After wiping my eyes and blowing my nose, I managed a smile.

"Today, Price. Today is for you. Today is for us. Show me your island."

CHAPTER SIX

Price

An unexpected fire drove me as I led Kate down the beach a mile to where I'd pulled a dinghy up on the shore yesterday. Her eyes were wide, her arms tight to her sides as she watched me tug it toward the shallow waves.

"This isn't the boat, right?"

I laughed heartily. "No, sweetness. It's out there." I pointed to the boat anchored several meters from the shore.

"Oh," she said.

Maybe a good night's rest had made the seemingly impossible predicament we were facing seem surmountable. Waking up to Kate's perfect mouth wrapped around me might have helped too. But damn, I had hope today that I hadn't had yesterday. Despite Kate's mini-meltdown over the omelet she did ultimately make— her best yet—today felt like a fresh start in some ways.

So far I'd maneuvered around her probing questions, and I was determined to deliver a day of simple happiness—the kind we used to have on any given day. God knew we both deserved it.

"In you go." I lifted her into my arms, carried her until the water was up to my thighs, and lowered her into the boat.

She scooted to the side, gripping the plastic handles tightly. I pushed the boat farther out before jumping in myself and yanking the propeller into action. In less than a minute I had us sidled up to the back of the boat. We'd made the journey between her space and mine, and somehow that brief transition gave me more hope still.

"My God, it's enormous," Kate said, her tone filled with awe as she looked up at the two-story vessel.

I laughed as I lifted her onto the back deck. "It's all right."

"You said it wasn't much. I wasn't expecting this."

I shrugged and hoisted the dinghy up onto the stern. "She's only a sixty-footer. Hanging around boat harbors in Maui and the Riviera puts things into perspective, I guess. Anything flashier would draw attention. Last thing I need is people asking questions about the guy on the yacht."

She trailed her fingertips over the black block letters circling the life ring that hung on the back. "Was she always named *Katherine*?"

I stepped behind her, hugging her against me. "If she were, I would have paid the seller his asking price," I murmured, nuzzling her hair and breathing in her fruity scent.

"I doubt it. Expecting you not to negotiate is like asking you not to breathe." She looked over her shoulder at me, intrigue sparkling behind her blue eyes. "Isn't it bad luck to rename a boat?"

I shrugged. "Not if you christen the new name properly. It's a process. You have to remove every trace of the old name from the ship before you bring anything with the new name on. Took me a couple weeks to get everything. I even had to throw the log books out."

I remembered those several days vividly. I hadn't been in a rush. After all, I'd had nothing but time since the crash. Stripping the vessel of its old identity had been oddly cathartic. I didn't have to guess as to why. Still, I'd brought Kate's memory with me, through everything, like a tattoo on my heart. A constant reminder of what I'd lost.

"What was she named before?"

"Shh." I lifted my finger to my lips with a crooked grin. "She's *Katherine* now, and she's served me well, so let's not jinx it." I took her hand, threading our fingers together. "Come on. Let me show you around."

I toured her through the few rooms of the boat—a master and a guest room, a basic kitchen and living room. I studied her expression all the while, looking for some sign of hesitation or uncertainty. All I could sense was that she was taking it all in. She'd always been the consummate observer, a true journalist at heart.

"So you live here...all the time?"

I razored my teeth along my bottom lip, weighing her words. "I do. I mean..." I brought my palm to the back of my neck and squeezed. *Shit.* I had to offer her more than a nomadic existence on a used boat. "You deserve more than this. I know that. This worked for me, but—"

She came up to me, resting her fingers over my lips. "Hush. That's not what I was trying to say. I asked out of pure curiosity. You can pretty much guess what this past year has been like for me. It was our life...just without you in it. I don't know anything about the life you've been living. Don't read into everything, okay?"

I exhaled with a nod. "Right."

She took my hand with a squeeze and brushed her lips against mine, the barest kiss. "Are you going to show me how to drive this thing or what, Captain?"

I smiled broadly against her lips. "Hell, yeah, baby."

I led her to the top deck and buzzed around, getting everything ready for an afternoon cruise around Leiloa. Kate took a seat on one of the couches flanking the captain's chair as I revved the engines to life.

"Where are we going?"

"You'll see," I teased. I swiveled and caught her by the ankles, lifting them onto my lap as I steered. Touching her even in the smallest way gave me comfort beyond measure. That connection kept my hope alive over my doubts.

"You aren't going to tell me?"

"You're just going to have to trust me." I gave her foot a little squeeze.

She giggled and tried to squirm away, but I kept her trapped.

"Leiloa is small, but it's full of hidden treasures. I'm going to show you a few of my favorite spots. Some you can only get to easily by boat."

She nodded, and even when I shifted my focus back to the waters ahead, I could feel her stare on me. I caressed up and down her calves, growing hard at the simple contact, but I had to stay focused on the trip and the long day I had planned for us.

"I did a little reading about this place before we arrived."

I lifted an eyebrow with a smirk. "Why am I not surprised?"

My mind conjured a vision of Kate doing her research after Chelle dropped the last-minute travel plans on her. She would stay up half the night reading articles and digging up information she'd need for a story. I'd find her hunched over her laptop, grooves marking the space between her eyebrows, so engrossed in her work she'd let hours go by without a break.

"Did you know in Samoan, Leiloa means 'lost'?"

My smirk faded a little. I met her thoughtful stare. "I did know that, actually. Hopefully it stays lost too. Only a couple thousand people live on the island. It's so out of the way I can't imagine it'll ever get built up and overtaken by tourists at this rate."

She frowned slightly. "How long have you been here?"

I shrugged. "A few months. I've never stayed anywhere too long, actually, but I like it here. Doesn't get more 'in the middle of nowhere' than an island lost in the Pacific."

She was quiet a moment before speaking. "A lost island for a lost man."

I tightened my lips into a flat line, because how could I argue? I *had* been lost—lost until Chelle brought my wife back to me. I'd be lost again if she left. Forever lost. Even so, I wasn't sure if I'd be able to bring myself to leave the island knowing that we'd made our last memories here.

"Where were you before?"

I thought of the laundry list of places I'd landed on my way here. I'd never felt settled or especially safe anywhere since leaving Kate that fateful night.

"I hid out in Europe for a while. Small towns in Switzerland. Then I made my way down to Italy and through Asia. I kept going south until I hit water. When I got a chance to hitch on a boat heading to Hawaii, I took it. I got to know the islands there well. That's when

I bought *Katherine* and started exploring islands farther out."

"I think I'm jealous." She looked down at her lap, twisting her fingers. "Chelle was right about that trip to Spain. Nothing could fix what broke inside me when you...*died*, but getting out of New York and filling up some of that emptiness with a new place and new discoveries helped somehow. Made me think I should do more traveling. Maybe it would help me move on. But when I came home, it didn't take long for everything to start to feel hopeless again." She offered a weak smile. "I'm sorry."

"You're fine. For better or worse, right? I couldn't be there with you, but I'm here now and I can listen. I know it's not the same, but I want to hear it if it helps at all."

She nodded, and I followed her stare out to the horizon. I wanted to hold her then, tell her everything was going to be okay now. I wanted to tell her over and over how sorry I was for everything I put her through.

The rhythm of the waves beating against the boat stilled my thoughts, letting them drift to happier times, when our love was simpler.

I smiled when an old memory floated over me. "Remember when we used to talk about Bali?"

Kate's eyes glittered with recognition, the corners wrinkling as she smiled. "Of course, I remember. What ever happened to that plan?"

I laughed and slowed the boat as we neared an alcove where I was hoping we'd spend the first part of the afternoon. Leiloa was just the kind of tropical paradise we'd talked about when we were two broke college kids. Then real life sucked us in and took over.

Our dreams of spending a few years living in a shack on the beach were swallowed up by job hunting and then the non-stop rhythm of life in New York City. Once we found our footing, all I could think about was making more money to buy us a bigger place in a better neighborhood. Somewhere we could raise kids, host dinner parties, and impress our families who'd mortgaged everything to put us through college.

"Just because it's an old dream doesn't mean we can't make it come true," I said, my tone hopeful.

I didn't look for her reaction, because the fear of her rejection still scared the shit out of me. But I wanted her to know it wasn't too late. I could still show her the world. We could find the kind of paradise we'd dreamed of.

◆ ◆ ◆ ◆

The falling sun marked the nearing end of a perfect day. We swam and snorkeled. We stopped into a little beach shack on the opposite side of the island for the best kalua chicken I'd ever tasted. We drank beers and remembered stories from our old life together. We laughed, and every time I heard that sweet music, I thought my heart would break from sheer joy.

I wanted Kate back in my life for my own happiness, but the promise of restoring hers took hold of something deep inside of me. It made me want to strip her of the choice and demand she stay, for her sake and for mine.

We sailed on to a tiny remote beach with the most beautiful blue-green waters I'd ever seen. She laughed when I chased her across the sand, finally reaching her only to haul her into my arms and kiss her breathless. We must have kissed for an hour under the shade of a smattering of palm trees whose umber trunks bent as they reached for the sea. I would have made love to her there too, but I didn't want to wipe her out before we'd finished our day.

If only every day could be this way. If only Kate could see this as our future. The two of us. An endless horizon.

My skin felt warm and tight from the hot sun on us all afternoon. Underneath, my muscles were relaxed, satisfied from the day's exertions. I wasn't quite ready to head home and let sleep take me, though. We were still a couple miles away from the place where I'd anchor *Katherine* for the night. Ahead of me, Kate was perched on the bow, her chin rested on her folded arms as she gazed out at the sea. Her legs were tucked under her, giving me the perfect view of her ass.

If nothing else, today completed the visual fantasy I'd had about this life with her. She didn't know yet that saying yes would mandate her to wearing bikinis for the foreseeable future. The same way I never wanted a moment to go by without touching her, every minute not being able to see and appreciate her physical beauty was a wasted one.

I slowed the boat to a stop, turning us so we faced the setting sun. I joined her a few minutes later, sinking into the cushion beside her.

"Hey, beautiful."

She moaned softly, leaning her head to one side. "Today was so perfect. It's like I've died and gone to heaven."

I trailed the back of my fingers along her arm. She didn't know heaven yet. Heaven was our bodies coming together while the sun sank into the horizon, nothing but the waves and the ocean breeze kissing our bare skin like a fine warm silk.

When our eyes locked, I cupped her cheek and led her lips to mine. I still hadn't tired of her mouth or the way our tongues stroked and dueled, a sensual dance we both knew well. As we kissed, I let my hands roam. Unhurried, I grazed over the pale pink triangles covering her full breasts, up the smooth column of her throat. When I found the tie of her bikini at her neck, I pulled it, baring her breasts for me.

She covered herself with her hands. "Price, we can't."

I slipped my hand between her thighs, dragging the tip of my thumb along the front center of the bikini bottoms. "Why not, sweetness?"

She released a small sigh and looked toward the island. Any curious humans would be the size of ant from this distance.

"Because..."

"It's just you and me, Kate." I took one of her hands away and wrapped my mouth around her nipple, enjoying how it beaded almost instantly under my tongue. I licked and nipped, plumping her breast in my hand, thanking God once again for creating the perfect woman for me.

"Are you sure?" Her voice was light, almost getting lost in the breeze that billowed over us. She bucked her hips to the rhythm of my teasing strokes against her clit.

I could make her say yes to anything right now. I licked the underside of her breast and blew a puff of air over her nipple. Her skin pebbled with gooseflesh.

"You want me to stop?" I slid the small scrap of her bottoms to the side, and before she could answer, I slid two fingers inside her. She was so ready for me, her cunt gloving me like wet velvet.

"No," she whimpered. "Don't stop. Don't ever stop."

Her eyes were half-mast, her breaths coming fast and shallow through those perfect lips. She reached for my shoulder as if to straddle me. Slipping out of her, I rose before she could. With my hands on her hips, I levered her forward. She took hold of the metal railing that framed the bow and spread her knees apart a few more inches.

I suppressed a groan of anticipated pleasure at the invitation. Straight ahead, the sun was a pinpoint of white light dropping toward the iridescent water. I made quick work of her bikini ties and positioned myself behind her. Releasing my cock from my trunks, I dragged the tip up and down her slit. The slow journey was the best kind of torture. My blood ran hot from my sun-scorched chest to the head of my aching cock as it met her clit, dipped along her drenched opening, and trailed all the way up to the star of her ass. I bit my lip, lingering. I'd have her there again. Soon, but not tonight.

Instead, I sank into her pussy the second the sun disappeared from view, its legacy a warm orange and pink glow stretching across the heavens. When she cried out, I thrust again, skimming my palms over every inch of my own personal heaven. The elegant angles of her shoulder blades as she held on through my thrusts. The narrow river of her spine flowing down to her tailbone. Those two perfect little dimples that fit my thumbs as I hauled her hips back, driving our bodies together in the most intimate way.

"So beautiful," I rasped.

I knew the slopes and valleys of this woman's body by heart.

She belonged to me, the same way I'd always belonged to her. The thought of another man ever having this view, or having already had it...

Fuck. That single thought cut straight through the haze of my pleasure. I sank my fingers into her flesh and punched my hips forward until I felt the resistance of her cervix against the head of my cock. Her knuckles whitened around the rail, but she didn't stop me.

My next thrusts were hard and fast. Possessive and fevered. Love, jealousy, regret, despair fueled each one. Her cries degraded into throaty moans and breathless curses, echoing and disappearing over the water until I could feel her nearing climax.

Stay with me. Be with me. Let me love you this way forever.

Every minute since I'd given her the offer, I'd wanted to get on my knees and beg her to stay. I couldn't get the words past my lips, though. Only one sentence would form, one plea that held all the others.

"I love you."

I said it over and over, under my breath, through gritted teeth as her velvet cunt tensed and tightened around me. My own release took me under, and I jetted inside of her, claiming her in the only way I could for now.

CHAPTER SEVEN

Kate

I love you.

Price's words echoed in my mind as I hurtled toward another orgasm. He'd never been quite so rough with me, but I understood his need and his passion. I shared them. I felt every thrust, every convulsion as he emptied into me. The metal railing gnawed into my waist, but I didn't care. He could have me. All of me. I was his.

"Mine," he said against my neck as if reading my thoughts. "Mine. My Kate."

As I fluttered downward, back into my mind, still he held me, his hands squeezing my flesh. We stayed still for a few moments, until finally I could go no longer without looking into his eyes. I tried to nudge him away.

"Price."

"Mmm." His groan vibrated against my neck.

"I... I need to...move."

He released me, and I turned, looking down. My skin was red and swollen where he'd gripped me as he pounded into me. Our passion had always been off the charts, but never before had he left a mark on my body.

Before he could notice and say anything, I gazed into his dark eyes. Something new was there. Something I'd never seen before.

"Price. What is it?"

His gaze fell to my hips. "Oh, God. Baby, I'm sorry."

"For what?"

"Did I hurt you?" He gently caressed the red bar across my waist.

"That? No. That was just the railing."

"Here?" He fingered the slightly raised welts on my hips.

I cupped his stubbled cheek. "It's okay. I'm fine. But what's going on? Something happened. Something made you go all...feral."

I put my bikini back on while he secured his trunks around his hips and then threaded his fingers through his dark hair, closing his eyes for a few seconds. When he opened them, his eyes were glassy. I'd never seen Price cry. He got misty every once in a while, but never had I witnessed an actual tear river down his cheek. Until now. It threatened to cut my heart into pieces.

I thumbed it away. "What is it, babe? It's okay. I promise."

He shook his head. "I have no right to ask you this."

"You're my husband. You can ask me anything."

"No. Not this. I gave up my rights a year ago. I couldn't expect you to..."

"To what?"

He rubbed at his temples. "I just can't stand the thought of it. Makes me want to—" He brought his fist down on the metal railing. "Damn!"

My pulse quickened. Price was fairly even-tempered. At least he *had* been. God only knew what he'd been through this past year. Maybe he was ready to tell me some of it.

"The thought of what?" I reached toward him and glided my fingers up his forearm. "You can tell me. You can tell me anything. Maybe it's time. Tell me what happened."

He let out a haunted laugh. "You have no idea."

"I'm sure I don't. But I will after you tell me."

"I mean, you have no idea what's bothering me. And I have no right to let it bother me."

I entwined my fingers with his. "You're talking in riddles, Price. Just tell me what's wrong."

He led me to a padded bench on deck and we sat down. He played with my wedding ring on my left hand, turning it around on my finger. "You're still wearing this."

I smiled. "We're still married, aren't we?"

"I'm glad we got platinum instead of yellow gold. It's perfect against your fair skin. And it lasts forever."

A lump lodged in my throat. I'd put the ring on my left hand for this vacation, but what Price didn't know was that I wore it on my right hand when I went to Spain. Oddly, it had been Michelle's idea. She'd convinced me it was time, that it was the first step in getting on with my life. Of course, that was before she knew Price was alive.

I cleared my throat and said simply, "It's always been a beautiful ring."

"Not as beautiful as the woman who wears it." He brought my hand to his lips and kissed my palm. "There's something I need to know."

"Of course. What?"

"I was gone a year, baby."

"Believe me. I'm well aware of that. The worst year of my life."

"I know. I mean, I hope it was." He shook his head. "Shit. That sounds all wrong. The last thing I ever wanted was for you to hurt."

"I understand." I wasn't sure I did, since he hadn't told me the whole story yet, but he looked so tormented I had to appease him. I couldn't stand that he was hurting.

"Like I said, I have no right to ask you this, but I have to. Call it a shortcoming of mine. Kate...was there anyone else?"

A rock landed in my stomach. How could I have had no idea that was coming? There hadn't been—not really. How honest could I be? Would my little flirtation in Spain matter to him? For that was all it had been—a few laughs and a few kisses—and Price had never left my mind. I'd learned the hard way that I wasn't ready yet to move on, that I was still very much in love with my dead husband.

Who wasn't dead after all.

He looked into my eyes. "Oh my God."

"What?"

"I can still read you. Tell me. Please." He closed his eyes. "Rip the bandage off."

"Has there been anyone else for *you*?" I asked.

"Of course not!" He stood, his cheeks reddening even in the dusk. "I've been running and hiding, trying to keep from getting killed, trying to set up what could be a life for us. When the hell would I have had time to fuck someone else?"

I straightened my spine but didn't stand. Jealousy. That's what I'd seen in his eyes that had never been there in the past. We'd never been jealous of each other. We'd always been secure in our commitment. In our love.

I heaved a sigh. If I expected him to be honest with me, I would have to offer him the same courtesy. I secured my bikini, walked toward him, and caressed his shoulder.

"Come back and sit with me," I said.

He gazed out to sea. "Do I want to hear this?"

"I don't know. You tell me." I squeezed his upper arm, which was tense and rigid. "I promised you today would be just for us. I agreed not to pester you with questions, and I haven't. Do you still want me to answer your question?"

"Damn. Yes. I need to know."

He followed me back to the bench where we both sat down again. I took his hand.

"First, I promise, I haven't been with anyone else. Not intimately."

He barely concealed a sigh of relief. "Thank God."

"But there was someone who pursued me. It happened during the trip to Spain."

He nodded tersely, his countenance still rigid.

I swallowed, gathering my courage. "His name was Alejandro Dominguez."

Price winced.

I covered our joined hands with my remaining hand. "He was..." I closed my eyes. The truth was, he'd reminded me much of Price—the same size, same coloring, same dark and smoky eyes. "A lot like you, actually. In looks and in personality. He was a reporter covering the protests, so that's how we met." I paused, giving him a moment to adjust.

"Go on," he said through gritted teeth.

"He asked me to go for a drink, and I said yes, just because I thought I could get him to share some sources with me. His English was excellent, which was good, because as you know, my Spanish is a little rusty."

He nodded, still tense.

"Still, I hesitated, but when he called me Catalina—Spanish for Katherine—I decided to go. The name made me feel like someone else, and someone else might go, right?" I gave a nervous laugh. "That probably sounds like nonsense, but being Kate had brought me nothing but sorrow for so long. It seemed like a good idea to be someone else. Anyway, I figured it wouldn't hurt to get to know him. We talked a lot about the story, but we also talked about other things. He was recently divorced, and I told him I was widowed. We shared a bottle of Rioja and ate seafood paella at this little dive he called a 'hidden gem.'"

I left out that I'd tasted food for the first time in months that evening. The crispy edges of the paella, the succulent scallops and clams, the sticky rice flavored with saffron—all had been heaven for my taste buds. The wine had been full-bodied yet fruity, perfect with the spicy dish.

I sighed. "He made me laugh, Price. And I hadn't laughed in so long. So when he..."

"When he what?"

"When he"—I winced—"invited me to his place—"

Price squeezed my hand hard.

I drew in a deep breath. "Remember, I thought you were dead."

He loosened his grip a bit. But only a bit.

"I considered it. He seemed like a nice guy, and I liked him. But I decided it wasn't good judgment to go to a stranger's home in a foreign country. So he walked me to my hotel, and he"—*just say it, Kate*—"kissed me."

Price's vise grip clamped my hand once more.

"I tried to respond..."

I paused, remembering. Alejandro's kiss had been nothing like Price's. And suddenly I realized why the paella and Rioja had tasted so good. I'd been fantasizing that Alejandro was Price. I'd focused on his dark beauty, and I had gotten past his Spanish accent, his designer clothes that Price would never be caught dead in. But the kiss. I couldn't get past the kiss. While there'd been nothing inherently wrong with Alejandro's kiss, and I might have found it pleasant under different circumstances, it was completely different from Price's kisses. Most importantly, despite my physical attraction to him, I hadn't felt anything—no passion, no desire, not even a spark of lust.

I wasn't Catalina. I was Kate, and Kate was in love with Price.

"But I couldn't, Price. It felt all kinds of wrong. So I apologized, thanked him for the dinner, and went to my room alone."

Alejandro *had* tried to change my mind, indeed had gotten quite persistent. My husband didn't need to know that. It wasn't important, anyway. The other man had eventually taken no for an answer and gone on his way. I returned to my room and placed my wedding ring back on my left hand where it belonged.

Though we'd exchanged email addresses, I hadn't heard from Alejandro since.

Gradually, Price loosened his grip on my hand. "Is that it?" he asked gruffly.

I nodded. "That's it."

"Good. Never again, okay?" His eyes were still dark with jealousy, still glassy with unshed tears.

I touched his cheek, reveling in his warm, scratchy stubble. This was a promise I could easily make. "Never again."

He stood, scooped me into his arms, and traipsed down the stairs to the master bedroom, where he laid me gently on the queen-size bed. "No one else," he said, more gently than I expected. "No one but me touches this beautiful body of yours." He traced my lips with his index finger. "No one but me kisses these lips."

"No one but you." I closed my eyes as his mouth came down upon mine.

The kiss was passionate and sweet at the same time—the cementing of two bodies and two souls who had been lost without one another. He slid his hands downward and removed my bikini top while I wriggled out of the bottoms. His cock pressed against me through his trunks, and I smoothed my fingers over his hips, pushing the garment down, lingering my touch on his warm skin. When we were both naked, he entered me gently, no foreplay other than our kiss.

Sweet, smooth perfection. I was always ready for him. Would always be ready for him. My body would forever be home for his.

I could have climaxed quickly, but I held off, as did he. We had transcended beyond simple need, lust, desire. This was only love. Pure love. Together we savored it as he slid in and out of me, letting the intensity build gradually. Our gazes never strayed from each other's, and in Price's I saw—not just with my eyes but with my very soul—all the love I felt for him mirrored back at me.

When our climaxes emerged in tandem, our lips met as we erupted together.

We stayed joined afterward, turned on our sides, our slick bodies melded together. Price breathed heavily against my neck, and I inhaled his spicy fragrance. All island, sea, and man.

"I love you so much, Kate."

"I love you so much too. Only you, Price. Forever."

He pressed his lips to my cheek, and I closed my eyes. This would be our bed. We'd always had a king-size, but there was limited room on the boat. Queen-size would keep me closer to Price, which was fine, because I was never letting him out of my sight again.

If I stayed, that was.

If I stayed...

If...

Who was I kidding? I could never leave—

A vibrating buzz interrupted my thoughts. Price kissed me quickly and then rolled to the nightstand to retrieve his cell phone.

His eyes widened slightly when he saw the screen, but he didn't take the call. Instead, he stood and pulled his trunks back on. He went to the small closet, took out a cotton shirt, and covered his bronze chest. Then he turned to me.

"We have to go. I have to dock the boat for the night."

"Who was that on the phone?" I asked.

But he'd already left the room.

CHAPTER EIGHT

Price

Otis had better have a damn good reason for interrupting my time with Kate. Deep down, I hoped he didn't have a good reason, because that would mean something was really wrong.

Otis was about a decade my junior—an island kid with a little too much drive for laid-back island life. He must have sensed the overworked New Yorker in me when he first found me in Maui. Not long after I'd purchased the boat, he nominated himself as my first mate for as long as I'd have him. He taught me about boats, and I taught him about stocks. He stayed out of my way for the most part. I didn't need the company, but having an extra set of hands around didn't hurt, and he'd more than shown me his value. I hadn't felt the need to tell Kate about him, because if she decided to stay, Otis would be finding a new gig and he knew it.

I went back to the helm and turned the key in the ignition. My phone buzzed, and I fished it out from my pocket. He was calling again. This time I answered.

"Otis, what the fuck do you want?"

"Bryson, buddy."

The sound of my alter-ego's name scraped against my nerves in the most unsettling way. For the past twenty-four hours, I'd been Price Lewis again. I wasn't in a rush to be anyone else. Price was the name on Kate's lips in the throes of passion. Not Bryson Carr. And certainly not that fucking Alejandro guy.

"Hey, I'm sorry—"

"I told you not to call unless it was important," I snapped.

I didn't want to be pulled away from Kate. Not now. Not ever.

"I know. I know. I thought this might be important, though."

Otis's slightly squeaky voice dragged me out of the rabbit hole of jealousy I'd fallen into earlier.

"What is it?"

"There's been some activity around the villa," Otis said, his words coming quickly. "I've been driving by the property a few times a day like you asked. Yesterday was clear, but there's been a black car with tinted windows parked down the road from the main gate all day. It's still there."

"Shit." I dragged my hand along my unshaven jaw as my thoughts whirled. The boat hummed steadily, breaking through the waves as we neared the place where I'd anchored last night.

"What should I do? Should I see who it is or—"

"No," I said firmly. "Stay away. Whoever is in the car could be dangerous."

"I can just play dumb groundskeeper or something. It's no big deal. How dangerous can they be?"

"Shoot-you-in-the-head dangerous, Otis. You know that as well as I do. Stay the hell away. I'm on my way back to the villa now." I exhaled a curse when I remembered Chelle. "My sister's there. Do me a favor and go check on her. I'll see you there in twenty."

"Sure thing, boss."

I ended the call and tried to quiet the wild racing of my heart. An unidentified car was parked on the boundaries of the remote beachside estate I'd chosen for my reunion with Kate. It could be a coincidence and absolutely nothing.

Or it could be my worst nightmare.

I jumped when I felt Kate's touch. Her hands curled over my shoulders and massaged into the tight muscles there. Nothing was going to get me to calm down right now, though.

"Everything okay?"

I shook my head.

"Who called you?"

"A friend," I said, my tone intentionally curt to keep this conversation short.

She took the seat on the couch beside me again. Furrowing her brow and crossing her arms, she studied me. "I'm not going to keep begging you to open up to me, Price."

I avoided her penetrating stare. "Good, because I'm not ready to talk right now. Sit back and let me get us home." I had to get us back to the villa so I could get to the bottom of the situation and rule out any threats.

She stood, her hands fisted by her sides, the line of her jaw tight before she spoke. "Today was amazing, Price. I felt like I was falling in love with you all over again. Remembering everything that made us great together. Until now, I'd almost forgotten what an asshole you can be when you want to be."

I sighed and reached for her hand. "Kate."

"Forget it." She evaded my touch and walked away, disappearing to another part of the boat.

I couldn't exactly run after her and get to our destination at the same time. I settled for cussing under my breath, dropping anchor the minute I spotted the villa, and hoping to hell I could turn this day around.

◆ ◆ ◆ ◆

Kate marched ahead of me toward the villa. I could tell by her pace and posture that she was gearing up to impose one of her royal silent treatments on me. She could work herself into a pissed off frenzy all she wanted. I wasn't spending a second of this trip in a stand-off with her. We didn't have that kind of time.

"Kate. Kate!" I jogged until I caught up with her.

Catching her arm, I turned her toward me. She yanked it back and crossed her arms, a perfect pairing with her pursed lips.

"I know you're upset," I began.

Her nostrils flared slightly. "Really. How could you tell?"

"Because you're indescribably beautiful when you're pissed off. Also, I'm your husband, and I know your moods before you do."

"I'm thrilled that you're so enlightened, Price. Can you also tell that I'm not in the mood to be left in the dark right now? Can you intuit that maybe I'm not interested in being treated like a naïve little woman who can't be trusted with the truth in order to make life-altering decisions about her future...with her *partner*? That's what we had, remember? An equal partnership."

I bit the inside of my mouth to keep from shouting back. This wasn't deciding on a house or signing on a loan together. This was life and death. She'd never faced death the way I had, so she couldn't understand.

"Kate, listen to me—"

"No, you listen to *me*." She unfolded her arms and pointed angrily at me. "I can't live like this. I *won't* live like this. You either tell me what happened to you and who's after you, or the answer is no. I love you and I'd rather die than leave you, but I won't spend the rest of my life living in fear because you can't tell me the truth."

She touched her hands to her chest, over the place where I'd pressed my ear so many times to hear her heart race after we'd made love. Tears glistened in her eyes, and I silently begged her not to cry. Her tears gutted me. They also guaranteed my defeat in any argument.

"You broke my heart, Price. Ever since I came here, I've been open with you." A tear fell as she opened her trembling hands like the pages of a book. "I opened myself to you in every way. Why can't you do that for me? Why can't you trust me?"

I raked my hands through my hair, biting down on the truth. It was too soon. I had to wait for her to say yes and commit to our new life together. But what if she wasn't bluffing? What if she said no because I was intent on keeping her in the dark?

"Kate, I'm trying to protect you. You have no idea what I'm up against here. These people have no humanity. The less you know, the better."

"I can handle it, Price. For God's sake, I've faced death. Do you understand that? I faced yours, and then for months I looked in the mirror and faced it all over again. Every day I had to make a choice. To keep going or to let the grief destroy me. I know you've been through hell. Even when you hide the truth from me, I can still see it in your eyes. Mine was a different kind of hell, but don't doubt for one second that I lived it too."

I dropped my gaze to the empty space between us, crushed by her admission. Someone physically ripping my heart out of my chest would have felt better than contemplating that I was the cause for Kate considering taking her own life. But that was grief. All-consuming, viciously painful, a dark plague stronger than any sense of reason. I knew it all too well.

"I'm so sorry. You'll never know how much."

"Talk to me, Price." She took my hand. "I'm begging you for the last time."

I swallowed hard and squeezed her hand. "I just need to know that you'll stay with me. I wanted to give you time to think it through. I didn't want to rush you into making such an enormous decision on the first or second day. You deserve a choice."

She shook her head, and I was certain my heart stopped beating.

"Please." I could barely hear the plea as it left my lips.

"Price, if you want me to stay with you and leave everything and everyone else behind, I will. I was ready to say yes when you asked me. But we need to walk into that future together, eyes open, with both of us knowing what challenges we might face."

Several seconds passed between us. I drew a deep breath of salty air into my lungs, both desperate and terrified to break the silence with the truth.

"I didn't know that last night in our apartment would be the last time I'd see you. I knew that things might be different when I came back, though."

She winced, but I continued before she could start probing again.

"I'd told you that I was going to Zurich for a conference. That much was true. But I didn't really go to network. I went there specifically to meet with one company, Cybermark Enterprises. I'd been watching them since I was day trading at Berg and Lynch. They specialized in data mining and were growing quickly, but not quickly enough to warrant the numbers I was seeing. After I broke off on my own, I kept following them. My system was showing that they should be growing exponentially, yet their stock price kept remaining steady."

"Maybe your system was wrong. For this one stock, I mean."

"Believe me, I thought of that. But my system has a ninety percent success rate. You know that. Plus, this company's prospectus and annual reports seemed to validate my conclusions." I shook my head. "I just couldn't let it go. I had to dig deeper and figure out why it didn't work with my math. When I reached out to them, I hinted about the trends and that I was interested in learning more about them. They offered me a job."

She lifted her brows. "You went there to interview?"

"Not really. I went there under the guise that I would interview. They met me under the guise that they were going to consider me for a job. We both had other plans."

My lips tightened as chaos filled my thoughts. Memories of the worst panic I'd ever felt welled up inside me. The roller coaster from hell designed to take me plummeting to my death was permanently etched inside my brain.

"They offered to fly me down to their headquarters in Geneva on a private plane to meet some of their executives. One pilot, one passenger. Single-engine plane." I shook my head with a grim smile. "It all felt wrong. The pilot could barely make eye contact with me let alone speak English. But I'd come all this way. I had to get to the bottom of it and figure out what was going on with these people."

"What happened? How did the plane go down?"

"We reached altitude and the pilot mumbled some shit in Italian. He put my hands on the controls and gave me the thumbs up like I was supposed to fly the goddamn plane."

Her eyes were wide now. "Are you kidding me?"

I shook my head. "Next thing I know, he's taking his jacket off and opening the door. He was packing a parachute and looking to jump. Guess who wasn't? Me."

She let go of my hand and brought both to her mouth. "How did you survive? The plane... The report said it was completely mangled. Burned through."

"That's because they filled the thing with so much fuel there wouldn't be a chance of finding a human body in it afterward or knowing one was missing. Doesn't matter because I didn't go down with the plane. I went down with him. I wasn't letting him leave that fucking plane without me, so I grabbed him. We tussled. The plane started to nosedive, and before I knew it, we were out of it, free-falling. Thank God he pulled the chute because I wouldn't have known the first thing to do."

"So you both survived. That's a miracle."

I shook my head. "Parachutes aren't designed to bring two grown men to the ground safely, at least not without serious injuries. We wrestled the whole way down, but I wouldn't let him go." I exhaled a shaky breath and brought the heels of my hands across my forehead like I could scrub out the horribly vivid memories. "Fuck. It was awful."

I walked to the edge of the water, letting the waves wash over my feet and sink into the doughy sand beneath. I'd never told anyone, not even Otis, what happened that day. Not another living soul knew my story. It occurred to me then that perhaps that's why the prospect of telling Kate had been so difficult. The ugly truth had lived inside me for a year, toxic and festering like a disease. Would telling her ease the pain? Soften the gruesome past?

I felt her arms wrap around my torso, her cheek press against my back. Some of the tension released with her touch. I covered her hands with mine, holding her tightly to me.

"We landed hard on the edge of a clearing. I broke my arm because I'd lassoed it through the shoot straps when he was trying to fight me off. But the way we landed... I was above him and my weight came down in such a way..." I swallowed over the nausea that hit me whenever the pilot's face beamed into my thoughts. The way the life left his eyes. The way his body tangled awkwardly in the chute. "His neck was broken. He died instantly."

We were silent for a long time, Kate holding me tightly, me breathing through the anxiety that hit every time I thought about that day.

"He tried to kill you, Price."

I stared listlessly out into the horizon. "I know. I tell myself that all the time. No matter how many times I have this conversation with myself, though, I never feel better about what happened."

She circled to stand in front of me, placing her hands on my cheeks. The same fierceness I recognized in her eyes earlier was there, but the context had changed.

"You saved yourself. And maybe it's cruel to say, but that man got what he deserved. You deserved to live, to come home to me, to have a life and a family. Never doubt that."

"I knew nothing about him. What if he didn't even have a choice?"

"Everyone has a choice," she said softly.

The sentiment resonated deeply. This past year had been a series of choices. One had ripped us apart, and others had brought us together again. I hoped that telling her the truth—well, most of it—tonight had been a good one.

"Now you know. And now maybe you can try to understand why I lie low instead of going to the authorities, which very likely would have gotten me killed, anyway. If they could pay a man enough to jump out of a goddamn plane, risking his own life to end mine, to what lengths would they go to take me out once and for all? When would it stop?" I took her hands from my cheeks and held them between us. "Then I thought about you and Chelle and my family. Kate, I swear to you, I just wanted to keep you safe. I've never experienced anything more terrifying than falling out of the sky that day, but if I'd put you in danger and risked your life, I couldn't have lived with myself."

Her bottom lip quivered as she spoke. "Thank you. For telling me, and for wanting to keep me safe."

"Baby," I whispered, reaching down to kiss her before her tears overtook her once more.

But before our lips could touch, a high-pitched scream came

from the direction of the villa. A woman's scream.

CHAPTER NINE

Kate

My heart was already stampeding from Price's story, and the cry coming from inside the villa forced it into a full-on gallop. Chelle was inside.

"Michelle!" Price turned and ran toward the villa.

I followed, fear coursing through me as I trudged through the sand as fast as I could. When Price reached the front door he threw it open.

"Michelle! Fuck, where are you?" He rushed through the living area, the kitchen. "Michelle! Chelle!" He grabbed two fistfuls of his hair.

My own nerves jumped hurdles under my skin. Chelle was my best friend. If something happened to her—

The back door to the villa opened.

"What on earth are the two of you bellowing about?" Michelle stood, barefoot, in a light-green sundress, her dark hair pulled into a high ponytail.

A young man with black hair, tan skin, and almond-shaped brown eyes—definitely from the South Pacific—entered and stood beside her. He wore flamboyant orange board shorts and a black muscle shirt.

"Otis," Price said. "What are you doing here?"

"You told me to check on your sister," the man said.

Price let out a heavy sigh. "So I did. God." He raked his fingers through his hair. "You two just took another year off my life." He rubbed his forehead. "Shit. What a stupid thing to say. I'm sorry."

I stepped forward, deciding not to comment on Price's lack of thought. He'd apologized, anyway. "We heard a scream. We thought..."

Michelle laughed. "Oh. That was just me. Your friend here walked right in on me. I had my headphones on, zoning out to some new age Zen stuff in that chaise over there"—she gestured to a leather chaise longue in the sunroom—"when I open my eyes and there's a strange man standing over me."

"I knocked," the man called Otis said. "I swear. But no one answered. I figured you'd want me to check things out. Why else would you have given me a key?"

"I'm regretting that," Price said.

I nudged my husband then. "Who is this?"

"Oh. Sorry. This is Otis, a friend of mine here on the island. Otis, my wife."

We shook hands briefly. "Nice to meet you," I said.

"And I guess you've met my sister."

"Yes," Michelle said. "After he scared the piss out of me."

My heart was still pounding from the ruckus. I was eternally thankful that Michelle was all right, but Price's story still rang in my head. I had so many questions, the first of which was why he hadn't introduced Michelle and me by name.

"After I assured her I was no threat, she pushed me out the door and gave me a stern lecture." Otis smiled.

A stern lecture? That wasn't Michelle. She had ripped him a new one. I couldn't help a subtle grin.

"Anyway, after he convinced me he wasn't a serial killer, we decided to have a glass of wine," Michelle said. "Want to join us?"

After the story Price had just told me, I wasn't sure wine would cut it. "How about a few shots of tequila?"

Price looked at me, his lips set in a straight line. "Since when do you drink the hard stuff?"

I didn't, usually, though Michelle and I had shared some shots one night a few weeks after Price's "death." We'd both been feeling extra low. The tequila, of course, hadn't helped. Only put off the inevitable.

"That sounds great, actually," Michelle said. "How about I whip us up some margaritas?"

"Do we have tequila?" I asked.

"The bar was supposed to be stocked." She walked to the bar on the far side of the living area and rooted around, coming up with a bottle of Patron Añejo. "Voilà!"

Michelle was in quite a good mood for having just been frightened out of her skin. But that was Chelle. Nothing bothered her for too long. Nothing that wasn't serious, anyway. Had she heard Price's story yet? Last night, I'd had the feeling he'd told her something, but she hadn't elaborated.

She began to cut up limes and shooed us out. "Go on out to the lanai. I'll bring the drinks in a few."

Numbness permeated my body. I wanted desperately to talk to Price alone, to ask him more about that fateful day that stole him from me. He hadn't told me everything. I could tell. How did he get care for his broken arm if he couldn't let anyone know who he was? How did he get here, across the globe, to this island? What did he do for money? He hadn't accessed any of our accounts since his "death." Did he tell anyone about the pilot's dead body? What about that company that was behind all of this? Why had he said the first night here that his parents, Chelle, and I would all be dead if that plane hadn't gone down? And who exactly was this Otis, and how much did he know?

I blindly followed Price and Otis to the lanai and sat down on a loveseat next to my husband. Otis sat across from us. He was young, early twenties at most. He should have been living in a frat house somewhere, ogling centerfolds and sorority girls. Why was he hanging around my husband?

I opened my mouth to ask, but Price spoke.

"I think you should go," he said to Otis.

Otis arched his dark eyebrows. "And miss the margaritas? Besides, your sister's hot, Bryson."

Bryson? I kept my mouth shut while Price went rigid beside me.

"My sister's too old for you."

"Hey, maybe she'd like a little cougar action with this willing cub."

Price stood, and I grabbed his hand, telling him without words to calm down. Thankfully, he did. He sat back down next to me, our hands still touching.

"Don't ever talk about my sister that way again."

Otis lifted his hands. "Sorry, dude. Hands off. I promise."

"I do need you to leave now. I need to talk to my wife and sister."

"After a drink? She invited me for wine, remember?"

"I don't give a rat's ass if she invited you to a gourmet feast. I need you to leave." Price's grip on my hand intensified.

The other man stood and brushed off his orange shorts. Some sort of understanding seemed to pass between them. Another question for my husband.

"Got it," Otis said. "Talk tomorrow?"

Price nodded, and Otis ambled down to a jeep parked nearby on the rocky road.

I bit on my lip. One thing was clear. Otis, whoever he was, knew a hell of a lot more than I did about what my husband was up to.

That was about to change.

"Price," I began, "there's a lot you—"

"Margs!" Michelle pushed the door open with her ass and walked out carrying a pitcher of light-green goodness and four martini glasses rimmed with salt. "All I could find. No margarita glasses."

I stood and took the glasses from her. "We'll only need three."

She looked around. "What happened to Otis?"

"He had somewhere to be," Price said.

"Oh, bummer. He was kind of cute."

"For Christ's sake, Chelle." Price shook his head. "He's a kid."

"What? I can't have a little fun? I'm supposed to spend three weeks alone while the two of you fuck like bunnies?" She poured our drinks.

"Not with him. Not that kind of fun, anyway."

Michelle rolled her eyes. "Fine. I was kidding, anyway. I agree. He's too young. Pretty nice to look at, though."

Otis *was* good-looking, but nothing compared to the man beside me...who still owed me a lot of answers.

I squeezed his forearm. "Price, how much does Chelle know?"

"Pretty much all that you do now."

"Yes, and I'm sorry I couldn't tell you, Kate," she said. "I wanted to, but he made me swear not to. It's a tough thing, having to choose between your brother and your best friend." She eyed Price. "Don't ever make me do that again."

"Believe me. I understand everything I've put both of you through, and I know a simple 'I'm sorry' is far from enough. And now..." He looked into the distance, his eyes glassy.

I stroked the top of his hand. "And now...what?"

He sighed. "Nothing."

"Price," I said, "don't lie to us."

"There's a reason Otis was here tonight. He's been watching the place for me for a while. I wanted to make sure it was out of the way enough so the two of you would be safe here. But..."

"What?" I said again.

"Otis saw a black car parked nearby earlier today. Did you notice anything, Chelle?"

"No," she said. "But I wasn't looking for anything either."

"What did you do today?"

"Walked along the beach for a while, lay in the sun and did some reading. I'd just finished dinner and was vegging out with my music when Otis came in."

Price let out a sigh. "Thank God. Maybe it's nothing."

But my heart lodged in my throat.

I had a feeling.

It wasn't nothing.

♦ ♦ ♦ ♦

I stared at myself in the bathroom mirror. I'd donned a see-through pale-blue teddy I'd found in the bureau. Price was in bed, waiting for me. I'd only had one margarita, and more questions flooded my mind.

He's been watching the place for me for a while. I wanted to make sure it was out of the way enough so the two of you would be safe here.

Out of the way enough? Exactly what did that mean? Was Price in hiding? Or was he not? Did someone know, besides Chelle and me, that he was alive? What was he keeping from me?

Ice forced itself through my veins, and I rubbed my arms.

"Baby?" he called from the bedroom.

His voice soothed me. This was my husband. Price. The man who would never harm me and would never let harm come to me. He'd said so himself.

Kate, I swear to you, I just wanted to keep you safe. I've never experienced anything more terrifying than falling out of the sky that day, but if I'd put you in danger and risked your life, I couldn't have lived with myself.

This was the man who loved me more than anything, as I loved him.

I inhaled deeply. "I'm coming."

I left the bathroom and walked toward Price.

"Wow." His eyes were heavy-lidded. "You look beautiful. That color suits you."

"You should know. You must have picked it out and stocked the dresser."

He smiled, his eyes shining with love, and my heart nearly melted. How could I question this man? This man who knew me so well? This man who loved me like no other? Who had risked everything to get back to me?

Still, the questions pounded on the door of my mind, demanding entrance...and answers.

Not tonight.

I wouldn't open that door tonight. He'd already shared a lot with me today, even after I'd promised to make the day just for us, with no questions.

I crawled into bed and snuggled up against him. He brought his lips to mine and kissed me slowly, sensually, until we were both writhing with need.

Then the kiss became more demanding. His tongue and lips stole my breath as he took from me, marking me again—if only in his head—as he had on the boat earlier. When we both needed a breath, he broke the kiss and inhaled sharply.

"Take off the teddy," he said, his voice leaving no room for disobedience.

I startled and met his gaze, his eyes burning. Normally he liked to undress me, peeling away each layer, whether slowly or quickly, as if unwrapping a gift.

Though I itched to question him, I kept silent, vowing once more to let him have what was left of this day together. I sat up and peeled the fine fabric from my body, pushing it over my hips and legs until it was no more than a puddle of sheer aquamarine against the bed.

"Now lie against me, spoon style," he ordered.

He didn't have to ask again. I loved spooning. I snuggled against his warm body, his cock meeting my lower back.

He kissed my shoulders, first gently and then harder, adding his teeth. I shuddered at the pleasure that surged through my whole body.

"You're mine, Kate. I've risked everything to bring us back together."

I closed my eyes, his words drifting over me.

"You promised." He nibbled at my neck. "You promised you'd stay."

I had. And at the moment, I'd promise him anything else he wanted. The feelings he was invoking in me, both physically and emotionally, were so compelling I was powerless to resist.

"Yes. I promised. I promise."

"I want to make you come, Kate. I want to make you mine."

I was already his. When he trailed his fingers over my arm to my hip, through the crease in my ass and began toying with me there, I stiffened a bit.

We'd had anal sex before, and we both enjoyed it. I wasn't sure I was ready to go there tonight, not when so many unanswered questions were whirling around in my head. Anal required trust of the highest magnitude. I trusted Price, but—

"That's it, baby. Let me in." He massaged me.

I tried to relax. Tried to remember how I once trusted him. How I *still* trusted him.

Within a few seconds, he breached the tight rim. "Easy, sweetness. Easy. This is mine. All of you. All of you is mine."

"Yours," I echoed.

Slowly he slid his finger in and out of me, and my pussy responded, aching to be filled.

"Price, please. I need you inside me."

"I *am* inside you, baby." He nipped my shoulder with his teeth.

"You know what I mean."

He moved backward a bit and slid two fingers inside my pussy. He moved them in the opposite direction as the finger in my ass. I sighed.

"I'm filling you up, Kate. That's me. Filling you up. Does it feel good?"

"God, yes," I whimpered.

"I want you to come, baby. Come for me. Right. Now."

Despite the lack of stimulation to my clit, I climaxed at his command, my hips undulating, pushing backward, trying to fill both my openings but still needing more, more...

I cried out when his cock filled my pussy.

"God," he grunted. "Wanted your ass, but couldn't wait..." He thrust into me hard.

Perfection. This was what I'd hoped for. He filled me, made me whole. My nipples pebbled as I clamped around him, took him into my body. I groaned into the pillow as my orgasm built again.

"Need you," he said gruffly, plunging deeper. "Need you, Kate."

Then he thrust deeply into me, filling me, and I came around him, hugging his cock with my convulsing walls.

"Mine," he kept chanting. "Mine."

◆ ◆ ◆ ◆

I jolted.

Price was still clenched against me. We'd fallen asleep after that last climax.

Something had woken me, but what? Moonlight streamed through the window. It was still nighttime. I couldn't see a clock from where I was—

A knock on the door. That's what had woken me. Chelle. I shivered. She wouldn't bother us unless it was important.

I left the bed, wrapped a sarong around my naked body, walked to the door, and opened it.

I gasped. Not Michelle, but Otis stood at the door. He'd traded in his board shorts and muscle shirt for jeans and a tie-dyed T-shirt.

"How did you get in here?" I demanded.

He held up a keycard. "I have a key, remember?"

"We have a phone, you know."

"It's important. I need to talk to Bryson."

Bryson. Right. Another question.

"He's asleep."

He walked past me into the room. "Not for long."

Price lay, his breathing shallow and even, the white sheet wrapped around his waist, thank goodness.

"He's not exactly decent," I said.

Otis was not deterred. He tapped Price on his shoulder, softly at first, and then more harshly. "Bryson, dude, wake up. We need to talk. Now."

CHAPTER TEN

Price

"What the hell is it?" I stared expectantly at Otis as I slid the door to the lanai shut behind us. The moon was still high in the sky. "What time is it, anyway?"

"Just past one in the morning."

I sighed, my muscles still heavy with fatigue. "This better be important."

"We had a visitor." He frowned, a grim expression darkening his youthful face.

I glanced around, my heartbeat ticking up as I readied for confrontation or danger.

"Not here, Bryson. Out there." He pointed toward the boat, whose starboard side faced us now. "I couldn't really sleep, but the boat was dark. I was just fucking around on my phone when I heard another boat getting close. I got up to see what it was, and the police were pulled up beside *Katherine* like they were getting ready to hop on and look around. I flipped the lights on and, honestly, they looked surprised to see me."

"What did they say?"

"When I asked them what they wanted, they said they'd had a report of suspicious activity and just wanted to check it out."

I frowned, running every possible scenario through my head. Leiloa was a quiet little island, and if anyone knew how to lie low, I did. "I have no idea what would warrant suspicion. I fucked my wife against the bowsprit last night. But we were at least a mile away from where anyone could see us."

Otis blinked a few times, his mouth agape. "That's hot, man. But yeah, I don't get the feeling that's what they were talking about. I mean, they had their fucking guns out like I was a drug runner or something."

"Did they search the boat?"

"Nah. They asked me a few more questions, like where I was from and what I was doing hanging around the island. I just told them the normal stuff. The truth with a bit of fiction, you know? They seemed satisfied, I guess, and then they took off. Weirdest fucking thing."

I scrubbed a hand down my face and paced around the lanai. Blaming my worry on a year's worth of paranoia would be reasonable, but something wasn't right. I could feel it in my gut, and my gut had kept me alive and out of trouble since that plane went down. After that day, I'd sworn I'd never again ignore my instincts.

"Something's wrong," I finally said.

Otis's lips thinned. "Yeah."

I dropped into a chair, rested my elbows on my knees, and looked to the ground. Fuck. We couldn't just have three weeks...or even one? Just a few more days of peace? Some time to figure out a plan for our future? Maybe even spend some more lazy afternoons exploring the islands? But no. This place was soon to be our past.

A cocktail of troubling emotions stirred in my veins. Dread and exhaustion fell heavy in my stomach. How could I do this to Kate? Had I really known until this moment what bringing her into my rootless life would be like? I pressed the heels of my hands to my eyes, as if I could stymie the flood of emotions there.

"Bryson..."

"That's not my name," I said shakily.

He was silent a moment. "I know, man. I know there's a lot you haven't told me, but I figure you have your reasons. Just tell me what I can do to help."

I shook my head in my hands. "I shouldn't have brought you into all this."

"It's all right, boss. I came to you, remember? And you know me. I like a little adventure."

Otis was young, still at that age where he considered himself invincible. Little did he realize this adventure could get him killed.

I looked up, a sudden appreciation for Otis and his unfailing loyalty tumbling over me. He was a good kid, and he could have a bright future. No way was I bringing him further into this mess. No one needed to know his part in it. I'd have to cut him loose. Sometime this week after I sent Chelle home and figured out how to get Kate and me someplace safer.

His duffle bag was packed full at his feet, like he was already preparing for imminent change.

"You can stay here tonight. Grab one of the empty bedrooms. We'll figure out a game plan tomorrow."

"Cool. Thanks, boss." He grabbed his bag, slid open the door, but paused at the threshold. "You coming in?"

I shook my head.

"You should get some sleep," he said. "We have no idea what tomorrow will bring."

"Thanks, Otis. I'll be in shortly."

He left, but I had no plans for sleep. Different scenarios pinged through my brain like rapid-fire. I always had contingency plans, at least a couple running at any given time. That was the nature of this new existence. But the possibility that the people who had tried to kill me really knew where we were had my adrenaline spiking like never before. In a few more hours, Kate and my sister would awaken. I'd need a plan for all of us.

I sat that way for hours, silently mapping our next steps. Before the sun rose, I took the dinghy out to the boat, retrieved some valuables from a safe hidden in the master bedroom, and packed a small bag. My personal items were few. Nothing held sentimental value anymore. Kate was my whole world, and our new life was about to begin.

She's going to leave everything behind for you. If you can't keep her safe, this was all for nothing.

My doubts tormented me as I worked in silence. By the time I made my way back to the villa, Kate had risen, though the sky was still dark. She stood on the lanai as I approached from the beach, her arms crossed and worry written across her face. I dreaded the conversation we needed to have.

"Where were you?" she asked when I joined her.

Instead of answering her, I pulled her into my arms and slanted my mouth over hers. She was tense, not resisting but not surrendering the way she had so easily yesterday. I flicked my tongue along the seam of her lips, but she wouldn't give in to me.

"Kiss me back, Kate," I whispered against her lips.

She turned her head, avoiding my lips and my gaze. Instead, I kissed her exposed neck, licking and nibbling at her skin until she shivered.

"Don't shut me out. I have to know you're with me."

She lifted her gaze to mine. "Shut you out? Every time you keep the truth from me, you're the one shutting *me* out. I've been lying in bed waiting for you to come back for hours. I searched the house and you're nowhere to be found. How is that supposed to make me feel? Where the hell were you? What's going on?"

"I'm sorry. I'm not trying to keep you in the dark. I just... I needed to touch you." I drifted my palms down her arms. "Otis woke me up to tell me the police tried to search the boat. There was a report of suspicious activity, supposedly. They left when they saw Otis was on board. But between the car and that, I'm worried about us staying here."

"Are you sure it's them?"

Them. The phantom word that represented Cybermark Enterprises, a multi-billion-dollar conglomerate who'd rather I were dead.

"I'm not sure of anything. But I'm not about to risk your life by being complacent. We should leave in the next twenty-four hours. I'll have Chelle change her flight as soon as she wakes up. Otis will ensure she gets off the island safely."

Kate swallowed hard but kept her jaw stiff like she was trying to be strong. "What about us?"

"How do you feel about Bali?"

She winced. "We can't stay here?"

"I'm sorry," I said, though I was certain my constant apologies were beginning to lose their potency.

"What will I tell my family?"

"Chelle will tell them you fell for a local guy and decided to stay longer. She'll feed them updates for as long as she can until we can have you reach out by email. We don't want to raise any suspicions about your safety and risk an investigation of any kind. So we'll come up with a story about this new life you've chosen, gradually close out your affairs in New York, and space the updates to once a year or so. Eventually they'll get used to the idea that you're not coming back. They'll think it's extreme, of course, but you had a traumatic loss and you've been suffering. They shouldn't be completely surprised that you fell hard for someone new and wanted to start over in a dramatic way."

Even as I said the words, I sent up a prayer of gratitude that Kate's life had not taken that turn. If she'd already given her heart to someone else... I couldn't even imagine it.

She stepped away from my embrace, wrapping her arms around herself as she stared out toward the sea. Tension lined her bare shoulders, and her fingers were pale from gripping her arms so tightly.

"It's better than faking your death, Kate. I didn't want to put Chelle in the middle of that story or your family through the grief. Plus, if Cybermark thinks I'm still alive, pretending you're dead isn't going to deter them, anyway. It'll just needlessly hurt the people you're closest to."

Several minutes passed as she stood in silence. I'd have given anything to have a line in to her thoughts, but I didn't want to push her. She was already fragile, and I'd just dropped a lot on her.

"How will we live...with no money? No identity?"

"I have plenty of money."

When she turned toward me, tears glistened in her eyes. "How? None of our accounts were touched after you died."

I sighed and geared up to tell her another unwelcome truth. "I had an account you didn't know about."

She squared her body toward mine, her lips parted slightly. "What?"

"The only good thing about falling out of a plane outside of Zurich was its proximity to the Swiss bank account I'd set up a few years ago. I'd opened it not long after I started working for myself."

Kate's hands fisted into tight balls. "How much was in it?"

"A few hundred thousand. It's not what you think, though. I wasn't trying to keep money from you. It was meant to be a nest egg. A safe one, in case anything went down with my work."

"Were you doing anything illegal?"

"No, Kate. Jesus." I cursed inwardly. "It's not unusual in my line of work—"

"It's not unusual to keep three hundred thousand dollars hidden from your wife in a Swiss fucking bank account? No, that sounds totally normal to me."

"Well, thank God, I did. Otherwise I'd have been a dead man emptying his bank account. Or I'd be working odd jobs off the books somewhere just to get by. Instead, I was able to pull the funds out and buy a new identity."

"Bryson."

I nodded. "Bryson Carr. I'd rather be Price, obviously, but it was close enough that I could get used to someone calling me a different name." I shoved my hands in my shorts and scuffed the bottom of my bare feet against the decking to fill the awkward silence. Once I got Kate off this island, I never wanted to talk about any of this shit again. "I used the money to buy you a new identity too. Passport, birth certificate, social security card. Anything we'd need...just in case. None of that came cheap."

Her bottom lip trembled slightly. "And who would I be?"

"You can be Kate as long as this story holds. If it doesn't, you'll still be my wife. Bethany Carr."

She turned away again, keeping her expression hidden from me. Bethany was the name of her oldest friend. They'd grown up together. She'd been Kate's maid of honor, and even though distance kept them apart, they had always stayed in touch and kept up the friendship. Still, I couldn't help but feel guilty, having chosen a name without her. I hadn't had any other choice.

Hell, I just needed her eyes on me. Her touch. Some reassurance that we could still do this. I started toward her, but she raised her hand to my chest before I could embrace her. The firm pressure on my sternum halted my progress, though her strength was no match for mine.

"You don't want to be kept in the dark, Kate, but—"

"I want to go back to New York," she said, her voice watery but firm.

I sucked in a breath, but my chest wouldn't expand enough to fully accommodate it. "Kate. No. Please."

"We can't live this way."

I curled my hand around hers, even as she took another small step back. Goddamn, she was going to make me beg.

"Kate, they may have followed you here. Once you're off the grid like I've been, we won't be running like this. I promise you. I want a good life for us. Something safe and stable. I want children with you and a home, preferably one that doesn't float. A place where we're not always looking over our shoulders."

"You can't promise me that."

Her words stung like the lash of a whip. They were undeniably true.

I'd been traveling the world as a dead man. I'd been running, but not from anything more than my own fear and misery. I couldn't guarantee her any kind of stability if bad people were intent on finding us.

I was running out of promises I could keep. But what about her promises?

"You promised you would stay with me."

"I know." She pulled her hand away, casting her gaze to the ground.

No. No. No. This wasn't happening. I couldn't lose her.

"So that's it? You expect me to just let you walk away?"

In an instant I knew I could never let her say no. I'd convinced myself that the choice to stay would be hers. The truth was I would fight for her until my dying breath, and I was about to fight dirty if it meant keeping my wife.

"I expect you to give me time to figure this out. I'm a journalist for heaven's sake. I don't put pen to paper until I know all the facts.

You're spoon-feeding them to me, just what I need to know, and now you expect me to jump when I don't have the whole story. I'm not giving up my life—*our* life—until I know we've exhausted all other options."

"What other options? Do you think if there were any other way I wouldn't be running like hell in that direction?"

"I think you've convinced yourself that you can't win this fight. You could expose these people and what they're doing. Let me help you find enough damaging information to take them down before they can hurt either of us."

My eyes went wide at her insane suggestion. "Go *after* them? Hell, no. Do you want to get us all killed?"

"Information can be more powerful than greed and malice."

I let out a short laugh. "Don't be so naïve, Kate."

She slapped me across the face.

Fucking hell. I feathered my fingertips over the sting on my cheek. Heat rose to my face and a kind of electric energy coursed through me as I chased the right words. She was wrong. I was right. She was being stubborn and altruistic and blind to the reality we now faced. She had no goddamn right to go back to New York without me. She was mine. We belonged together.

I could say it all damn day, but I'd rather show her.

"You're not going to New York without me, Kate."

The muscles in her jaw tensed as I took a step closer. I caught her wrist and yanked her toward me. I held her tense frame against mine, giving her no room to consider putting space between us again. I was mad as hell, but our bodies together felt perfectly right. Nothing would ever change that.

Fire burned behind her bright blue eyes. "You don't get to tell me what to do. You lost that right when you left me."

"You were always with me, everywhere I went. Haunting me, breaking me, and keeping me alive all at once."

She closed her eyes with a wince. "Stop."

"I won't stop. I'll never stop loving you. Needing you. Fighting for you." I slid my palms down to her ass, caressing and squeezing her bare bottom through her sarong until she was pressed firmly against me. "Fucking you," I murmured against her parted lips.

I brought my hands to the front of her sarong and parted the swaths of fabric that hung like a curtain over her bare curves. I cupped her breasts, kneading their fullness and gently pinching her pert nipples between my fingertips.

"Price. Not now."

"Yes, now."

I pinched harder until she gasped, closing her eyes against the pleasure I knew it gave her.

"You're threatening to leave me, and I'm going to show you why that won't work."

"I'm not—"

I didn't let her finish. I pressed our lips together, taking advantage of the interruption to swipe into her mouth. I groaned into her when our tongues met.

Within ten seconds of feasting on her, I was hard as granite. Ready to take both of us straight out of this reality and into a better one. I'd lived inside fantasies of being with her for so long. Having her here, in my arms and in the flesh, was still too miraculous to fully comprehend. Didn't matter how pissed she was with me.

Hoisting her up against me, I held her up by the thighs and carried her toward the house. Her back met the solid glass of the slider while I took her mouth in another uncompromising kiss. As I contemplated the door, I decided the bedroom was too far. I had to have her now.

"Hold on, baby," I rasped, guiding her arms around my neck with one hand.

Then I pushed down my shorts and guided my cock into her. Something about our fight must have turned her on because she was fully aroused, gloving me with ease. I rutted deeply and she cried out, digging her fingernails into my shoulders.

"Damn you, Price," she groaned.

Nothing about that deterred me. Her passion and her anger only fueled me. I smiled and thrust harder. I owned her pleasure. Only I could take her where we both needed to go—to another world where the past year hadn't come between us.

I held our bodies together and pumped into her like a piston, fucking her with abandon toward an orgasm I now desperately needed. She sliced her fingernails across my skin, cursing me and moaning my name. I retaliated by fucking her harder.

"You're so deep. So hard. It's so good."

I used all my strength to lift and slam her down onto my cock over and over. My muscles burned. My cock throbbed. I couldn't be inside her more completely. The pressure was dizzying. But the way she trembled against me told me she felt it too. All of it. Every solid inch of my possession.

"Are you going to come for me, sweetness?"

"Yes," she whimpered. "So close."

"Who do you come for?"

"You, Price. God, only you."

"That's right. Come for me now. Just like that. Show me how good I make you feel."

In an instant, she was there, coming apart in my arms. Her pussy locked around me until I was certain she couldn't be any tighter. The helpless cries that left her lips pushed me over. My lover. My wife. My everything. I found the deepest part of her and let go, releasing with a satisfied groan against her skin.

I didn't want to let her go, but my legs were growing weak in this position. I slipped from her and lowered her to the ground, holding her steady as we transitioned from one person back into two. When my brain cells started firing normally again, I remembered what had brought us here. My face didn't hurt anymore, but my heart would be in serious trouble if Kate tried to run off on me. Hopefully we'd closed that conversation down for now, though.

I caressed her cheek, thumbing over her freckles and following the defined angle of her jawline. So beautiful. I bent and kissed the corner of her mouth.

"Hit me again like that, Kate, and I'll fuck you so hard, you'll feel me for a week."

"That doesn't sound so bad." She sagged against the door with a sigh, her eyes fluttering open and then closing again. "And anyway, you had it coming."

CHAPTER ELEVEN

Kate

I couldn't quite wrap my mind around the fact that I'd slapped my husband—the man who meant everything to me. I'd never done anything like that before—never even thought about it, no matter how much he was impersonating an asshole—and to do so when our lives were upended as they were...

But yes. He'd had it coming, calling me naïve.

I might be ignorant of the facts—and that was his fault, not mine—but naïve? He'd called me innocent two days ago during our first walk on the beach. Funny, it hadn't affected me the same way, then. Now I knew he was deliberately withholding information, and as much as I loved my husband, I couldn't forget that. If I was going to stay with him—and God, I wanted to be with him more than I wanted my next breath—he'd have to offer up all the facts. My heart was strong, but I could no longer keep my head out of this equation.

Price interrupted my thoughts. "I'm only trying to protect you, Kate."

I opened my eyes. "Why not let me help protect *you*? Protect *us*? Tell me what we're dealing with. The whole truth. Let me in. I feel so helpless, Price."

"Baby—"

"We took vows, remember? For richer, for poorer. In sickness and in health. For better or for worse."

"You don't understand."

"Would you stop saying that?" I balled my hands into fists. "The only reason I don't understand is because you're not leveling with me. For better or for worse, Price. If this is worse, I promised to help you through it."

"This goes so far beyond worse."

I shook my head. "Doesn't matter. Just because we didn't foresee how bad something might get doesn't invalidate the vow I made to you. You made the same promise to me."

"I did, and I'm trying to keep that vow. I'm trying to protect you."

I gave him an angry glare. "Wrong."

He jerked his head. "What?"

"If you were truly trying to protect me, you would have stayed hidden, let me live out my life safely in New York. As soon as you involved Chelle and me in this, protection ceased being your goal."

"That's not true. I—"

I placed two fingers over his full lips. "I didn't mean to sound quite so harsh. I'm not blaming you. I'd have done the same thing. The thought of a life without you...even if it meant protecting yours..."

I could accuse him of being selfish for wanting me with him, but it didn't ring true. My life during the past year, without Price, hadn't been a life at all. If I'd thought, for one second, that I could be with him again, I'd have risked everything. Yes, I would have done everything I could to keep him safe, but in the end, still knowing that the safest thing would be to stay hidden, I'd have taken the risk.

That's what he had done. He'd chosen a life with me over my ultimate protection. I didn't begrudge him that—though maybe I should have—but he had to understand the reality of it.

"Kate..."

"It's okay. You weren't being selfish. You were just being...*you*. I can no more live without you than you can without me."

He sank his head into his hands. "My God. I never thought about it that way. But you're right. I'm so sorry, baby. I'm so fucking sorry."

I pulled him toward me, removing his hands and cupping his cheeks. "Don't be sorry. Just understand that this is what it is. I'm all in now. You have to let me help."

"I know what you're going to say," he said.

"Oh, you do?"

"You've already said it. You want to go back to New York."

I nodded. "I do. Otherwise we'll always be running. Always looking over our shoulders."

He gripped my upper arms, his eyes ablaze in the light of the dawn. "You want the truth? The whole truth?" He sighed. "The truth is that going back to New York could very well get us both killed."

I swallowed the lump in my throat. He'd already told me as much, but still the words lanced through me like a hunting knife. I didn't want to die. But I didn't want to spend my life running, either. What kind of a life would that be? I'd be with the man I adored, yes, but I could never bring a child into that world. I'd never be a mother, never see my belly swell with the fruit of Price's and my love. I could give up my career, my family, my friends. But could I give up the chance to have children?

Words formed in my throat, and I had to force them out. "Price, from what you've said, we could end up getting killed, anyway."

Price raked his fingers through his hair. "I know how you get when you want to know something. You persist and you persist. I understand, but baby, could we go to bed, please? I've been up most of the night. Right now all I want to do is hold you. I need to feel you in my arms."

I hadn't slept any more than he had, and I was feeling it. Perhaps we could both look at this a little more objectively if we were better rested. Michelle wasn't an early riser, so we had several hours before she'd be up. Spending those hours snuggled up to my husband sounded like a pretty good idea. Without saying a word, I took his hand and led him inside to our bedroom.

I hadn't planned on making love again—we both needed sleep— but when he undressed me and began kissing me, all bets were off. He slid into me without hesitation, and as he filled me more deeply, I closed my eyes and gave myself up to the moment.

Whatever happened from here on, I was happy Price had brought me to the island. My life would never be the same, but at least we were together. Even if we had only these few hours, they were better than a lifetime without my soulmate.

His thrusts became harder, and I lifted my hips to accommodate him. As I glided into orgasm, he nipped at my ear.

"For better or for worse," he whispered.

"For better or for worse," I echoed.

◆ ◆ ◆ ◆

I rolled over on the bed to touch my husband...but found only emptiness on his side of the bed. "Price?" I sat up and looked out the window. Bright sunlight streamed in.

I got up, went to the bathroom, and then put on a silk robe and slippers. I padded down the stairs to the kitchen.

"Hey, sleepyhead," Michelle greeted me.

I looked around. "Where's Price?"

"He and Otis left a while ago. He didn't want to wake you up. Said he wouldn't be too long."

"How long ago was that?"

"A couple hours."

"Shit," I said under my breath. I'd hoped we could talk through everything once we had some sleep. "What time is it?"

"A little after noon." Michelle pointed to her plate. "You want a sandwich or something?"

I shook my head and opened the refrigerator. Nothing sounded appetizing, but I took out a bowl of fruit salad.

I gasped when the front door opened. Price walked in, sans Otis, thank God. Maybe now we could talk.

I ran into his arms. "Where have you been?"

"Just taking care of a few things."

"What things?" I didn't care that Michelle was within earshot. She probably already knew more than I did.

"Just things, baby. Nothing for you to worry about."

I met his gaze head on. "This stops now. Everything is something for me to worry about until you assure me otherwise."

He opened his mouth, but I stopped him with a gesture.

"And no. Just you saying it's nothing for me to worry about won't cut it."

"Come to think of it," Michelle said from the kitchen, "I agree with Kate. Let's get it all out on the table. This 'vacation' hasn't been anything like you promised, big brother. It's time for you to spill the beans. Are you in trouble?"

Trouble? Michelle knew he was already in trouble. Why else would he have faked his own death and be hiding out on a tiny island?

However, Price eyed me with a slight shake of his head, so I said nothing to Michelle.

"Nothing more than you already know," Price said. "Excuse me for a minute, okay?"

He walked out of the kitchen and toward Michelle's bedroom.

"That was strange," Michelle said.

I nodded. Strange didn't even begin to describe the happenings of the last few days. I scooped fruit salad into a bowl, sat down next to Michele, and took a bite of papaya. "Is there coffee?"

"Yeah. I'll get you a cup." She rose.

"Thanks."

A few minutes later, Price returned. "I have great news for you, Sis," he said to Michelle. "Otis has volunteered to take you sightseeing and snorkeling today."

"Huh?" Michelle widened her eyes. "After your 'not with him' comment yesterday?"

"It's not a date. Don't worry. But I know you've been stuck here for two days without much to do."

"I wasn't complaining. The beach is right outside."

"I know. But wouldn't you like to do something else?"

"This was never about me, Price. This was about you and Kate. I'm happy to do my part."

"Well"—Price cleared his throat—"today is about you. I want you to have some fun while you're here." Again, he met my gaze, his eyes pleading.

Was I supposed to talk her into this? That's what he seemed to be indicating. I'd always been able to read Price well.

"Why don't you go for it, Chelle?" I said. "Price showed me all around the island. It's wonderful. There are some cute little shops where the local artists sell their work. You love that kind of stuff. The food is amazing too." I turned to Price. "Make sure Otis takes her to get that great shaved ice we had."

"Are you sure you two will be okay?" She let out a raucous laugh. "I can't believe I just said that. You're going to christen every inch of this villa, aren't you? I guess I can't blame you for trying to get rid of me."

"I'm not trying to get—"

Michelle stopped Price. "I was kidding. I'll go. It will be nice to get out. I'm going to shower and change. When is he coming?"

"Soon."

A knock sounded at the front door.

"Very soon, apparently." Price stood.

"Shit. Tell him to give me five." Michelle charged to her bedroom.

I followed Price to the door. He opened it and let Otis in.

"Hey," Otis said. "Is my date ready?"

"It's not a date," Price said through gritted teeth.

"Easy, man. I'm kidding." He walked in and sat down in the living area. "Is everything in order?"

Price picked up a manila folder that I hadn't noticed sitting on a table by the door. "It's all in here, bud. I don't have to remind you that you're carrying precious cargo."

"I've got it. Honestly. You can count on me."

My muscles went rigid. What was going on?

Michelle came flying out of her bedroom wearing shorts and a tank top and carrying a beach bag. "I've got a swimsuit, towel, and my snorkel. Is there anything else I might need? Oh, wait. I didn't grab my passport."

"No need." Otis said. "You don't need ID on the island. They know me personally everywhere we're going. Best to leave your passport here where it's safe."

Michelle smiled. "Good enough for me. See you guys later." She followed Otis out to his jeep parked on the gravel driveway.

Price turned to follow them, but I grabbed his arm. "What's going on? What was in the envelope?"

He watched his sister drive away with Otis, an unreadable look in his eye, and then took my hand in his, brought it to his lips, and kissed it. "How about we take Michelle's advice and christen every inch of this place."

Lust surged within me, but we were so not going there right now. Not until I had some well-deserved answers. "No dice." I pulled my hand away.

"It was worth a try. Sit down and have a cup of coffee with me. I have a lot to tell you." He led me into the kitchen, topped off my coffee cup, and poured one for himself.

I sat, numbly, waiting for the truth to spill from his mouth. When seconds turned into minutes, I said, "It's your move."

He took a sip of coffee and sighed. "Otis and I went to talk to the local authorities this morning about the tussle at the boat last night."

"Yeah?"

"Well...it turns out, the locals weren't anywhere near the boat last night. Neither was the coastguard. No one had any record of the disturbance."

My pulse quickened. "What does that mean, exactly?"

"It means—or rather, we *think* it means—that whoever was searching the boat had disguised themselves as law enforcement."

I gulped.

"If that's true, Otis actually talked to..." Price rubbed at his temples. "It means they're here, Kate."

Icy chills spiked over my body. "They?"

"Hired goons, most likely. None of the principles at Cybermark would get their hands dirty."

Nausea threatened to overtake me. "What will we do?"

"We have some time. I had Otis leave a trail of bread crumbs that will keep them off of us for about twenty-four hours, if we play our cards right. Right now they're headed toward the coast of Japan."

That didn't make me feel any better. Twenty-four hours might seem like an eternity in some circumstances. Right now? It would be a flash in the night.

"Another thing, Kate." Price cleared his throat. "I'm only telling you this because I'd expect you to tell me if the situation were reversed. I nearly had Otis check out that Alejandro guy you told me about."

"Nearly?" A prick of anger hit me. Here we were, our lives in danger, and he was worried about my almost fling?

"Don't get pissed. I couldn't help myself. I just had to know."

"What stopped you?"

He sighed. "I'd like to tell you that I had a change of heart, but that would be a lie. We simply ran out of time."

"Oh, well." I still felt sick to my stomach. "Lack of time or not, I hope you realize we have more pressing concerns than Alejandro. He's a non-entity. He means nothing to me and he never did. Besides, what could Otis have found on him, anyway, other than a Google search? He's just a kid."

"He's a kid, yes. He's also a fucking genius. Why do you think I'm working with him? Most island guys his age are surfing and chasing beach bunnies with no thought of ever doing anything else. He's driven. He's brilliant. He's a gifted hacker. He's a genuine pain in my ass sometimes, but he's got a heart of gold and he's never let me down. I trust him. I trust him with my life...and with yours."

And then it hit me—like a deafening thunderbolt after the kind of lightning strike that illuminates a whole house in the dead of night. "He took Chelle."

He nodded. "Otis is taking her to safety."

"So what you said yesterday, about asking her to change her flight..."

"I had to scrap that plan."

"God, Price. What was in that envelope?"

"Several things. The title to *Katherine*. Otis is going to sell her for me and wire the money to us."

"And?"

"A detailed itinerary...and Michelle's passport."

"So when you left the kitchen..."

"I took her passport from the drawer in her bedroom and put it in the envelope."

"What if she had gone back to get it and found it missing?"

"Otis took care of that, remember?"

I dropped my mouth open. Then, "Did you have that all planned out?"

"No. Otis is just really good on his feet. I'm telling you, he's a genius."

Fear nearly kept me from giving voice to the next words lodged in my throat. "We're never going to see her again, are we?"

Price let out a heavy sigh. "It's possible."

"Oh my God." I rubbed at my forehead. "You went after her, but I grabbed you. I kept you from saying goodbye, didn't I?"

"It's okay, baby. I kept you from saying goodbye as well. We're together, and Michelle will be safe. That's what ultimately matters."

"Where is she going?"

"To a small island near Martha's Vineyard. When she gets there, I have instructions for her to call my parents and have them meet her. The three of them will stay there in a highly secured compound as long as necessary."

I breathed in and then out, trying to keep steady. "Martha's Vineyard?" Seemed a little too close to home, but how could I question Price and Otis? They'd been in this far longer than I, and Price would do what he thought best to keep Michelle and his parents safe. "You arranged all of this in a span of two hours this morning?"

"No. I've always had a backup plan. I've had to."

A backup plan...

Twenty-four hours...

Off the coast of Japan...

All feeling left my body, and my voice emerged, eerily monotonous. "Where are you and I going, Price?"

CHAPTER TWELVE

Price

The answer to Kate's question wasn't exactly simple. Especially now that she'd already expressed a desire to go home to New York. Where would we go? I could get us safely to Central America. Our new identities would ensure us safe passage out of the country. Otis had friends with properties trickled along the Pacific coast from Nicaragua to Peru. But what if Cybermark was still tailing us? Would any place be home for long?

My guilt went to war with my determination to keep Kate with me at all costs. When it came to planning our future, I'd taken complete control. I'd lived the past year unable to trust anyone. Not even Otis at times, out of pure self-preservation. But now Kate was here, by my side, seemingly ready for whatever challenges the future might bring. Maybe she'd been right to push back.

"Where do *you* want to go?"

She laughed weakly. "You're asking *me* now? I thought you always had a plan."

"Of course, I do." I dragged a hand through my hair before meeting her eyes again. "But I'm asking you what you want. We're in this together, like you said."

She hesitated, gauging me with a tentative look, like she couldn't believe I was really opening this door. I couldn't completely believe it either, but I was committed to prying one hand off the steering wheel and sharing control of the partnership, even if the prospect scared the hell out of me.

"Tell me what you're thinking, Kate."

She parted her lips to speak, a subtle pleading in her eyes. "I was telling you the truth last night. I do want to go back to New York, but I won't go without you. The thought of just running away from our life and never looking back terrifies me. It feels...*wrong*."

Dread fell like a stone in my stomach. Going to New York was possibly dead last on my wish list of next stops. "You realize how many problems that would pose? I'm supposed to be dead."

Her brows pinched a little, a tick that told me she was contemplating something.

"We don't have to tell anyone. At least not right now. Chelle knows, but she'll be away for a little while, anyway."

I shook my head. "So...what? I hide out in our five-hundred-square-foot apartment for the rest of our lives and hope no one with malicious intentions notices? Maybe that's a life for you, but that's prison for me."

She came to me and took my hands. "We wouldn't need to hide for long. Maybe not long at all if we go public about what you found."

Panic shot a thousand ice picks across my chest. "Jesus, Kate. It's all speculation. I mean, even if you had any of my old files, I'm not sure there would be anything there worth bringing to light. I went to Zurich to dig deeper and find more. Obviously that plan was thwarted. I couldn't ask anyone else to take that risk again."

"I'm a journalist, and I'm not alone. I belong to a network of people around the world who are dedicated to finding and reporting the truth. We could bring this to the top of the *Tribune*, or tap some of my contacts at the *Journal* for a story that would publicize what happened. An exposé that would protect us. We could reach out to people quietly at first—"

"Kate, no. Just *no*."

I couldn't listen a minute more. I walked away toward our bedroom. I slammed the door behind me and stared out at the lanai, my arms folded firmly across my chest. What the hell was I thinking, having her weigh in? I'd shut down the conversation earlier, and here we were again, talking about New York. The worst possible place for either of us. Then again, just because I got her to stop talking about it in the throes of an orgasm didn't mean she'd stop thinking about it forever. I could pretend she wouldn't resent me if I led her down this road of life on the run, but that wouldn't serve either of us in the long term. Shit, this was impossible.

I heard the door click quietly, and then the softest shuffle of her coming toward me.

She wrapped her arms gently around my waist. A minute or so passed with just sounds of our breathing, my loud thoughts dulling to a frustrated murmur in my mind.

"I wish you had more faith in me," she whispered.

I closed my eyes with a sigh. "That's not it. You're brilliant, Kate. I just..."

How could I make her understand? She was always the one with the gift for words...whether she was soothing or seducing me with them or twisting them around mine to get her way.

"Price." She pressed a warm kiss to my shoulder blade. "You've been running for a year. What they did to you and the choices you made afterward nearly destroyed us. This needs to stop. They need to pay for what they did. I'm not willing to sacrifice our life—the promise and security of our family—only for them to keep going on like nothing happened. What if you weren't the only one? Who else have they made a victim?"

Kate gave voice to thoughts I'd had more than once. Nothing had ever seemed worth inviting more of their violence against me or the ones I loved. We were no longer off the grid, though. So much had changed.

I lazily caressed her forearms as she held me tightly. Together... for better or for worse.

As long as we were together, we could get through anything. I had to make myself truly believe it. After all, I'd taken our other vows to heart. I'd been as loyal to her as she'd been to me. I had to trust in the rest of those promises, even if the unknown terrified me.

"New York then." My voice was barely a whisper.

Still, she'd heard me. I felt her nod against me. I swallowed back a curse and ignored the voice that screamed at me to run in the other direction.

"Okay, Kate. We'll go to New York."

◆ ◆ ◆ ◆

As promised, Kate and I had left the villa and the island paradise of Leiloa inside of forty-eight hours. While Otis was on his way to the Vineyard with Chelle, I'd arranged a private charter boat to get us back to the Honolulu airport undetected. Kate had looked like she might be sick checking in with our fake passports to avoid any trace of our return. I'd been more worried about staying in the sky on the long journey to JFK. There was a reason I'd stuck to boats and ground transportation since the crash.

Ten hours later, I held the armrest in a death grip as the 747 suddenly dropped in altitude. Sweat collected on my forehead as we descended through the clouds. A blur of heinous unwelcome memories played out in my head.

My stomach in my throat as the nose of the plane tipped toward the ground. The twisted smile on the pilot's face as he bid me farewell. The panic when I locked my grip on him, unwilling to accept death. The free fall. The full hour I spent dry heaving in the company of a dead man before I could find a way to treat my wounds. The beginning of the worst year of my life...

Kate covered her palm over mine, her sweet voice a salve over my rattled nerves. "It's okay, baby. We're almost there."

When the sounds of the engine changed and the landing gear dropped, another wave of nausea hit. I closed my eyes and blew out a small breath, comforted only by the promise that in twenty minutes we'd be on the ground.

Kate squeezed my hand a little tighter. "We're almost there. Almost home."

Only a few more minutes and I'd be in New York again.

I'd be home.

◆ ◆ ◆ ◆

The outskirts of the city were quiet. The chill in the air matched the dull gray sky. I knew the route from the airport to our apartment by heart, having taken it many times. Dozens of early mornings like this on the way to my next trip. Late night returns and the blur of city lights as I counted down the minutes until I could be with Kate again. This time we were coming home together, hand in hand, our hearts heavy with all that lay ahead.

Every mile, every step toward home was beyond surreal. The way our ascent to the third-floor apartment echoed loudly through the narrow stairwell. The yellowing paint on the railway that ended on the landing in front of our door. The bronzed "3B" nailed to the mullion. None of it seemed real.

As Kate searched her carry-on for the keys, I stared in silent disbelief and took in details I'd long forgotten. For everything that had been familiar—from the neighborhoods we passed on the way to the doorstep of our brownstone—somehow, I felt like a stranger, a fraud. I was supposed to be dead. How could I ever belong here again?

Kate bit her lip and turned the key in the lock, opening the door into my past. She shuffled in with her bags, and I followed. I had only a backpack slung over my shoulder, having learned to pack light on my travels. The smell of the apartment hit me first. That odd aroma that one notices in other people's homes, made up of detergent and pets and furniture and the people who inhabit a place. I wondered quietly what ours was made of and why it seemed so foreign to me now.

When the silence crept up, I found Kate staring at me, her smile tight and her eyes wide and tentative. "Everything okay?"

"Sure. I'm good," I said, trying my best to sound genuine, but my feet were frozen in place. Something about being here again had me paralyzed.

She shifted her gaze around the room. She chewed her lip again, her expression uneasy. "I'm going to grab a quick shower, and then I'll make us something to eat and clean up a little, okay?"

"Go ahead. I'll make some coffee."

She went to the bedroom and then disappeared into the tiny bathroom we once shared. I held my place just beyond the doorway, attempting to acclimate to the shock of being someplace I never thought I'd be again.

The modest interior of our place hadn't changed much. The furniture was arranged the same. A second-hand couch and my old worn recliner that I'd insisted on bringing from my apartment in college. A glass coffee table that we could never keep clean atop an ornate Persian rug her parents had bought us after their first visit. A few dead plants sat wilted on the windowsill. That's when I really noticed the clutter. Every surface seemed to be covered with mail, old magazines, rolled up Sunday editions of the *New York Times*.

Only then could I move. I walked slowly to the bedroom. Again, not much had changed except Kate's clothes were hung on every available hook and corner. Reminded me of when she couldn't decide on an outfit before some big party or event. The room would be a tornado of discarded garments. But Kate had always been a neat freak, a trait I was grateful for after years of college living with frat-house standards. The only tidy area of the room now was the side of the bed that used to be mine. The bed sheets were only rumpled on her side, as if every night she lifted them and tucked herself in carefully. As if an invisible person still inhabited the other side.

Emotion prickled in my throat. What had I done to her? How could she ever trust me again? I dropped my bag, stripped my clothes, leaving them in a pile on the floor, and went to the bathroom. I found her in the shower, her hands on the tile, her head bent under the hard spray.

"Kate."

She sucked in a breath and looked up. "Is everything okay?"

"Everything's fine. Can I join you?"

"Sure."

I stepped in and reached for the shampoo. "Have you washed yet?"

She cast her gaze low. "No, I was just thinking."

I squirted some in my hand and nudged her to turn so I could lather it into her hair. Her shoulders softened and her hands fell limp to her sides. I smiled when the smell of grapefruit filled the tiny room.

"Dare I ask what about?"

She sighed before speaking. "You've had a plan for us up until now. It's my turn to figure out what to do next. I know we have to be careful about who we approach and how."

"We'll figure it out, Kate. Tomorrow we'll come up with a plan."

I unhooked the sprayer and rinsed the shampoo until the water ran clear again.

She turned and gazed up at me, resting her hands on my chest. "You came here for me. I can't let you down. We should go through your files tomorrow. That's probably the best place to start."

I silenced her with a deep kiss that had her melting against me. Then I reached for the loofa and the body wash. Letting the silence settle between us, I washed her from her perfect breasts all the way down to her manicured little toes.

We'd made love so many times, but I still felt like I needed hours to properly reacquaint with her body. The truth was I needed forever. I hadn't even had a week.

Hell, she hadn't even gotten a chance to fully enjoy the three-week getaway Chelle had promised her. We'd been going non-stop since I stepped onto the beach several days ago, and such a small portion of that time had been truly restorative. The day spent exploring Lciloa hadn't been nearly long enough. I knew how to push my own limits, but I couldn't let the stress eat away at both of us the way it now threatened to.

I finished washing myself, turned the water off, and grabbed fresh towels.

She wrapped herself in one, went to the bedroom, and paused beside the bed. "God, I'm sorry, Price. This place is such a mess."

"Don't worry about it. I'll tidy up today. You should rest for now. We've been up for hours."

I meant it. The fatigue from the extended day tugged at me too. But after ten minutes of lathering up her luscious body in the shower, my cock had other ideas. I embraced her from behind and sucked her earlobe in my mouth. "Unless you want to mess up the other side of the bed with me, of course."

She smiled weakly. "It's weird. I know."

"Not at all." I reached for the knot of her towel and tugged until it fell to the floor. Pulling her against me, I reveled in the sudden heat of her skin against mine. Suddenly I wished we were back on the island. In the heat where clothes were optional and life was a little simpler. If only for a moment.

"I'm starting to believe that somehow you knew I would come back."

Her bottom lip trembled. "I wanted so much to believe that you would, even though deep down I knew it was impossible. The reality of you being gone forever was too painful to live with day after day. Sometimes I'd let myself fantasize that you were away on business. I'd pretend like I was just counting down the days until you'd come home again. I knew it was fucked up to think that way, but I couldn't help myself."

I grazed my hands over her warm skin until she shivered and pressed her ass back against me. Her damp hair dripped between us, making us slick as we pressed tightly together.

"I'll always be here, Kate. Right next to you. Every night. Always."

With a breathy sigh, she took my hand and guided it between her thighs. I found my mark quickly, stroking and toying with her clit until she was slick with arousal.

No way was I letting her rest. Not until I'd fucked her very thoroughly, the way I planned to every night for the rest of my life. How had I lived so long without the pleasures of her body, subsisting only on fantasies of how it had been between us?

She bucked her hips into my touch. "Price...I love the way you touch me. I missed you so much."

Craving more, I slipped my fingers deep into her heat. She moaned softly and rolled her head back on my shoulder. The angle gave me easy access to her neck, so I kissed and nipped her there, all the while fucking her rhythmically with my fingers.

"Did you ever touch yourself like this, sweetheart?"

Her pussy tightened around my fingers in that moment. "I tried not to, but I missed you so much. Missed the way you felt inside me. Nothing could make me come the way you did."

"What did you think about, sweetness? What was I doing to you in your fantasies?"

She was quiet a moment. "The last time...before you left. I don't know why. That whole day is still so vivid to me. I remembered wanting you to take me so hard that I'd feel you for days after you'd left."

I tugged her hips back against my erection with a groan. We'd fucked hundreds of times, but somehow our last time before the crash was indelible on my mind too. I wasn't sure I wanted to reenact the memory that was tied to so much heartache for the both of us, but it was good inspiration at least.

"Up on the bed, sweetheart. Put your ass in the air for me."

I withdrew from her cunt and slapped her ass as she walked away. She went without argument, situating herself in the center of our bed. She stretched her arms out in front of her and rested her head on the mattress as her hips angled upward in an erotic pose. I stroked my length a few times, pent up as ever at the sight of her perfect glistening pussy. I crawled behind her and pushed her hips higher so I could get easy access to all the places where I intended to pleasure her.

I caressed the backs of her thighs and spread her cheeks gently. She jolted when I slid two fingers past her quivering opening down to her clit. I teased her there a moment more before making the return journey, dragging her arousal up to the rosy pucker of her ass.

"Do you trust me, baby?" I added the faintest pressure against the tight muscle. Testing. Asking.

"Yes."

Even as she said the word, I felt her tense slightly.

"Then let go. Let it all go."

I bent my head and followed the path my fingers had taken with my tongue, once, twice, again and again until she writhed and pushed back against me with a needy cry on her lips. The tension in her body had changed. The tension was now made of need, the desire to be filled. And I couldn't wait a second longer to take her.

CHAPTER THIRTEEN

Kate

Price trailed kisses over the curve of my ass, up my spine to my shoulders and neck, making me shiver. His hard cock pressed between my cheeks.

I knew what he wanted—the ultimate intimacy, the ultimate show of trust.

We'd always enjoyed anal play, but now it seemed to have an even deeper meaning. He was asking me to trust him completely.

I always had in the past, and I did now. He'd shown me his ultimate trust as well, by coming back to New York with me. I vowed that his trust would not be misplaced.

"Take me, Price," I said softly. "I trust you."

He rubbed the head of his cock over my ass, further lubricating me with my own juices. "Ready?"

"Yes. Please."

He breached the tight rim of muscle.

I swiftly inhaled, adjusting to the invasion. Then he thrust all the way inside me.

So full. So full of my love. Such an intimate joining.

"Okay?" he said.

"Mmm, yes. More than okay." I pushed back against him.

"God, Kate." He pulled out and then plunged back in. "So fucking good."

I closed my eyes, relishing the fullness, his presence in my body. This was the one act we'd only done together, never with anyone else. Only Price had been to this private place within me, and only he would ever be. I reveled in the closeness, so visceral and real.

This was the essence, the very blood of life—love and trust reduced to pure physical form.

He pumped into me furiously, taking my hand and leading it to my clit where we massaged the hard bud together, he instinctively knowing the right rhythm, until I began to ascend into orgasm.

"That's right, baby. Make it feel good. Show me how much you love what I'm doing to you."

His words threw me over the edge, launching me like a catapult into beautiful oblivion.

"Price!" I cried out.

"Kate! God, Kate!"

He pushed into me with one last mighty stroke, filling me, our climaxes summiting together in a kaleidoscopic rush.

I never wanted to come down again.

◆ ◆ ◆

I awoke a few hours later in Price's arms, still in our spoon position. Night had fallen. I had no idea what time zone my body was in. I didn't even know what day it was.

I smiled, allowing the bliss of our joining to saturate me once again. I settled into the curve of his body, when a sound jarred me.

I widened my eyes. Price still snored softly next to me. I stealthily moved out of his cocoon toward the edge of the bed. I rose and put on the first clothes I saw, a pair of old jeans and a tank top. God, this place was a sty.

Slowly, my nerves a jumbled mass, I walked to the front door, flipped the light switch, and looked out the peephole. What I'd heard couldn't have been a knock. Anyone coming into the building had to use the intercom. I opened the door. A piece of paper sat on the floor. I looked around quickly and then picked it up, my pulse racing.

An advert for a local pizza place.

A heavy sigh escaped my lips. I'd gotten all worked up about a flyer. Some kid had probably been paid to distribute them inside the building.

But in the middle of the night?

I shook my head. Maybe the flyer had been there for a while and we hadn't noticed it before. After all, we'd been carrying our bags and looking over our shoulders when we arrived. Or maybe it had gotten shuffled toward our door by someone else walking by.

Still...what had I heard?

It hadn't been a knock, so what the hell was it?

Icy shivers ran through me, and I crossed my arms over my chest, trying to ease the chill. Were we safe here? I truly believed Price and I could get through anything together, but had I been wrong to suggest coming back here? I didn't want to keep running, but what had I gotten us into? If I'd put Price in danger—

I shook my head to clear it.

Could not go there.

I'd said it before. We were in this together now.

"Kate?"

I looked up. Price stood in the doorway of our bedroom.

"Hey," I said. "What are you doing up?"

"I woke up and you were gone. I've had too much of that this past year."

"I'm sorry." I laid the flyer down on the mail table and looked around the room. "I heard a noise."

Price stiffened. "What noise?"

"It was obviously nothing. I think I'm just on edge. I know it was my idea to come here, but I can't help it. I'm having second thoughts. I know we used the fake IDs and all, but still... Maybe we should go to the island where Michelle is, do our investigation from there."

"That's not possible and you know it. If we show up there, we're liable to put Chelle and my parents in danger."

"So your parents got there safely?"

He nodded. "I just checked my phone. I got a text from Otis."

Good old Otis. "And where is he now?"

"He's there with my folks for now, until we decide what his next move should be."

"We?"

"Yeah, we. The decisions aren't mine alone to make anymore. They're ours."

"And Otis is fine just waiting around until you tell him what to do?"

He smiled. "I pay him very well for his time."

Right. All the money I never knew my husband had stowed away. I stopped my hackles from rising. It was all water under the bridge now.

Now. That was what we had to focus on.

"You want to come back to bed?" he said.

"Yes, Price. I do. I want to go back to bed and lose myself in your body again. I want to forget about our reality and live in a fantasy world." I walked toward him, pulling at a lock of my hair. "Maybe I was wrong. Maybe we should have stayed on that island."

"That was no longer possible, baby. We had to go somewhere else. They had picked up my trail. They know I'm alive, Kate."

"We could have gone to Bali. To another tiny island somewhere. An uncharted one."

"On a three hour tour?" He smiled again, his dimples as gorgeous as ever.

I melted against his body, chuckling for a few seconds at the memories of sitting together in Price's old recliner, watching reruns of *Gilligan's Island* in college. But I quickly became sober again. "How long until they find you here?"

"I don't know. Could be weeks. Could be hours. I just don't know, baby." He stroked my head. "Come back to bed with me."

I nodded into his chest.

He undressed me and pulled me to him, kissing me gently at first, and then more passionately, sliding his tongue against mine. Price's kisses were magical. In his arms, I could escape anything, be only Kate—Kate who was perfectly safe with her true love.

He cupped my breasts, still kissing me, thumbing my hard nipples. I deepened the kiss, needing more intensity, more... everything.

He laid me on the bed and covered my body with his, trailing his lips over my cheeks, neck, shoulders...and then to the swells of my breasts. I arched into him, my nipples aching for his lips. He didn't disappoint me. He tugged one hard bud between his teeth while pinching the other between his thumb and forefinger.

I moaned, my pussy yearning to be filled. His granite cock pushed against my thigh, and I rubbed against it, eliciting a low grown from his throat.

"God, baby," he said against my flesh.

"I want you, Price." My voice was a husky rasp.

He let my nipple drop from his mouth and slid down my body, leaving soft kisses in his wake. When he got to my vulva he inhaled. "So ripe." Then he flicked his tongue over my clit.

I cried out, spreading my legs farther apart, reaching downward and grabbing a fistful of his silky hair. I ground into his face.

He devoured me with lips, teeth, tongue, fingers until I was reduced to a sobbing mass of jelly. One orgasm became two, two became three, until my entire body flooded over with a pleasure so intense I was almost in pain.

But oh, what pain it was. Perfect pain became perfect pleasure, morphing back and forth until I begged him to stop.

"Please, Price. Your cock. I need your cock."

He flipped me over onto my belly and pushed my thighs forward so my ass was in the air. Then he thrust into me, filling me completely. When his finger touched my asshole, I nearly exploded again, and when he breached the tight rim, I unraveled, my already sated body sinking into the softness of the bed as my husband penetrated me from behind.

My pillow muffled my cries and his thrusts increased.

"I love you, Kate. I love you so much."

As he joined me in climax, I sobbed his name.

"Price. Price. Don't you ever fucking leave me again."

♦ ♦ ♦ ♦

The sun streamed into our bedroom, waking me once more. At least it was daylight now. Price still slept. The poor man was exhausted. He'd no doubt spent the last year exhausted, always on the run, always looking over his shoulder.

I still firmly believed that was no way to live. So why did I keep having doubts?

Simple. As much as I knew the right thing was to be here, to be home, I wasn't ready to lose Price again. And the reality was that our lives depended precariously on how quickly we could come up with some kind of resolution to this situation—a situation I still didn't fully understand.

I crept out of bed, trying not to disturb Price, donned the same old jeans and tank, and walked to our small galley kitchen. Price and I had enjoyed cooking together on occasion. I smiled, remembering the time we'd prepared sushi completely naked and then eaten it off of each other's bodies. Neither of us was a master chef by any means, but we enjoyed doing almost anything together.

I opened the refrigerator. Not much there. What was left of a dozen eggs I'd purchased a couple weeks ago, some green onions that were now wilted, a moldy piece of cheddar cheese, and some ham that had seen better days. I threw out the last three items and then looked at the eggs. They were still decent. One of my not-so-famous omelets was out of the question, but I could prepare my husband some scrambled eggs. Later, I'd go to the market.

But first, coffee. I reached for the canister of beans. Empty.

Shit. How were we supposed to deal with all of this sans caffeine?

I could run downstairs to the little coffee shop on the corner and get some fresh-brewed goodness. No one was supposed to know Price was here, but *I* still lived here. Nothing wrong with me getting some coffee. After all, the whole reason I'd wanted to come home to New York was because I didn't want to live a life on the run.

I went quietly back into the bedroom and put on some shoes and socks, grabbed a jacket and a wad of cash out of my purse, and left.

The Kaphi House was run by a sweet middle-aged Nepalese couple, and they brewed a mean cup. I got two large coffees, a bag of beans, and a loaf of their homemade sweetbread, and then hurried home.

"Kate!"

Price was pacing around the living room when I entered.

"What? What's wrong?" I set down the cups and bag.

"Where the hell were you?"

"Relax. I just went down to the corner to get coffee. I'm fine."

"You shouldn't have left the apartment. What if someone had seen you? God!" He raked his fingers through his disheveled hair. "Someone *did* see you. Who was working today at the shop?"

I gulped. "No one. I mean, no one I recognized."

"Aaryan and Nina weren't there?"

"Maybe in the back. I don't know." I handed him the bag. "I got some of that bread you like."

"Jesus Christ, Kate. What were you thinking?"

"I was thinking I wanted a fucking cup of coffee! This isn't a huge deal, Price. Everyone knows *I'm* alive. Did you expect me to hole up in here forever? We need food."

Price grabbed the bag containing the bread and coffee beans from my hand and threw it to the floor. "Who was there? Who saw you?"

"Why does it matter? I'm a regular there. It would look more suspicious for me *not* to go. No one knows I went to the island other than you and Chelle." I retrieved the bag. "You've probably ruined the bread."

"Just answer me, Kate. Who saw you?"

"A new guy. He was young. Had an accent."

"You've never seen him there before?"

"No. Usually Nina is there in the mornings, except on weekends. What day is it, anyway?"

"Fuck if I know." Price plunked down on his old, ridiculous recliner. "I'm serious. What if someone had seen you?"

"Aaryan and Nina are my friends. They'd never do anything to hurt either one of us."

"They wouldn't? What if someone went into their shop and put a gun to their heads? Do you think they'd remember seeing you this morning?"

My breathing became rapid, but still I persisted. "They didn't see me. Their barista did."

"And you're sure he didn't know you?"

"I'm pretty sure."

"I need you to be damn sure."

"He didn't know my name. I didn't recognize him. It's fine, Price. I promise." I hoped I was right. What if I'd just made a huge mistake? For coffee? I cleared my throat. "Besides, it's just as likely that someone saw us when we came home last night. Or last... whatever it was."

"Don't leave the apartment without telling me again."

I sat next to him and cupped his cheek, fingering his stubble. "I'm truly sorry I worried you. But I have to leave the apartment. I need to go shopping or we'll starve."

"We'll have groceries delivered."

"We still have to answer the door and pay for them, especially if you insist upon using cash."

"Shit." He stood. "Why didn't I think of this before? I'll get Otis to arrange everything. We won't have to leave this place."

I smoothed his hair. "We can't stay in here forever. You know that as well as I do."

"This isn't like me. I should have arranged for food with Otis. I should have—"

I touched two fingers to his lips, quieting him. "You've had to do the thinking of about ten people during the past year. Don't beat yourself up for forgetting something as mundane as grocery shopping."

"This isn't like me."

I brushed my lips over his. "Let it go. I'm fine. No one saw me except the new kid working the front at The Kaphi House. Okay? He doesn't know me from Adam. I won't go out again without telling you. But Price, I *will* go out. Otherwise we're prisoners here."

He grabbed a fistful of my hair and tugged on it lovingly. "You're so brave, baby. You always were. But you still don't know what we're dealing with here."

"Yes, I do."

"You don't. And God, I wish you never had to find out."

I kissed him again. "Well, I do. For better or for worse, remember? Why don't we get started? I've got caffeine, sweetbread, and eggs for fuel, and we're going to need it if we're going to start digging through your files." I stood, retrieved the coffees and sweetbread, and took them to the kitchen.

Price followed me and sat down on one of the bar stools where we usually ate our meals. He took a long sip of his coffee and sighed. "I have missed this."

"They do make a great cup," I agreed.

"I just wish..."

"No one saw me. I promise. Do you want some eggs? That's all I have, other than the bread."

He shook his head. "Coffee is fine for now. I need to think."

"Okay." I pulled off a piece of the doughy sweetbread, inhaling its yeasty aroma. "While you're thinking, I'd like to take a look at your files. Where should I begin?"

He took another drink of coffee. "Most of them are on my computer and are encrypted. But I do have a hard file you can start with."

"Great. Where is it?"

He stood. "It's in the living room. I kept it hidden behind that old Melville anthology your father gave you. One book I knew neither of us would move from the shelf." He walked toward the bookcase.

I couldn't help a chuckle. My father was a Professor of

Literature at Brown, and he loved the classics. Other than Jane Austen, I wasn't a fan.

Price pulled the book off the shelf. "I installed a little safe behind here a while ago, a few months before my plane went down."

"And you didn't tell me?"

"I couldn't, Kate. Now you know why. I'm sorry."

I nodded. Though I did understand, I still felt a little sick every time I learned something new that Price had hidden from me. A secret bank account. Now a safe in our home. Not to mention the fact that he'd been alive all this time.

I stood behind him while he turned the combination lock and opened the narrow door.

Then I gasped.

He turned. "What?"

"I heard something." I looked over my shoulder. "Nothing."

"Christ, Kate. You scared the hell out of me."

God, my nerves were on edge.

He looked back to the opening, reached inside, and then faced me.

My nerves couldn't take much more of this. "What now?"

His face was white, his lips twisted into something I hadn't seen before. My heart leaped into my throat.

"Kate. Damn it!"

"What? You're scaring me."

"This morning. At The Kaphi House."

"We've been through that. Everything's fine. I won't go again without telling you."

"Everything's not fine." He banged his fist onto the shelf, hard enough that two books fell to the floor with a thud. "And you won't go again, period."

My lips trembled. "Why? What's the matter?"

"You got *two* cups of coffee this morning."

CHAPTER FOURTEEN

Price

My heart slammed against my ribs. The cool calm I'd always maintained when I was on my own seemed to have expired. Was it because we were back in New York? Was it because Kate was by my side, and I was risking her life now as well as my own?

Whatever it was, I clutched the thumb drive between my fingers, seemingly unable to control my paranoia. The urge to take the files, my wife, and my few personal possessions and flee the city was almost too strong to resist. Instead, I slammed the safe shut and replaced the book in front of it. I paced across the room to the window, anxiously shifting my gaze up and down the street, looking for something—anything to indicate that Kate's innocent excursion for coffee had compromised us. Parked cars. Expensive strollers. A homeless guy across the street. Everything seemed typical from this vantage, but I couldn't calm my nerves.

"Coming here was dangerous. We should leave."

When I turned, Kate's eyes were glistening and her lips were tight. She was upset...and angry. "We just got here, Price."

"We'll find someplace more inconspicuous than our fucking

apartment. I don't know why I didn't insist on it to begin with. Obviously this would be the first place they'd look. If they found us on an island in the middle of the Pacific, they'd find us here. Fuck!" I yanked the shade down and went to the bedroom in an angry huff.

"Price, stop. Let's think this through." Kate's footsteps followed behind mine. "We need a plan. Running every time we're spooked isn't a plan."

"Fine. The plan is to get away from the apartment. We'll stay in a hotel. Someplace with cameras and enough traffic to deter anyone who might discover where we're staying." I tossed on the T-shirt and jeans I'd thrown off last night and went to our closet, finding all my old clothes still arranged as I'd left them. Never thought I'd go clothes shopping in my own closet a year later, but here I was.

I grabbed a few garments and returned to find Kate standing before me, her eyes wide and misty, like she was about to see her whole life washed away...again. My heart hurt to see what this was doing to her, but bending around her feelings was putting us in danger. I'd give in to her until we were in the grave, but I wanted a lifetime with her first.

"Let's go." My voice was clipped.

Her lip trembled, her posture no less rigid. "I can't do this. I'm not like you. I can't pack my life into a duffel bag. This is my home. *Our* home."

I paused. *We can come back later. Chelle can send us your things.* Both were lies resting on my lips. Why feed her lies?

"You have twenty minutes. Then we're taking the train to Midtown. We may not be back."

Her tears spilled over, and I clenched my fists. I had to stay strong...for her. For us. She shook her head, her vacant stare passing over the clutter that we'd yet to clean up. We'd made a mess of this life. It was time to move on. Time to start fresh.

She walked over to the rumpled side of the bed that had been pristine before our arrival, grazing her fingertips over the bedspread. My side. Then it struck me. The apartment had become her shrine to the dead me. Asking her to leave it was asking for so much more.

I went to her, grasping her by the shoulders gently. "Kate, look at me."

She did, her blue eyes even bluer behind her tears.

"My home is with you, Kate. Not in some shitty apartment in Brooklyn. Wherever you are is where I can be happy and whole. I lost all my possessions, my identity, my whole life. But I held on to the one thing that was most important to me—you. I had you with me, in my heart. I have you now. We have each other. No matter where we go, that's always going to be the most important thing."

She nodded, another tear streaming down her cheek.

I brushed it away, wishing more than anything I could reach inside her and erase all the pain I'd ever caused her.

"Price?"

"What is it, baby?" I whispered, tucking a strand of hair behind her ear.

She swallowed and lifted her gaze to mine. "We can go. But..."

She tangled her fingers into my cotton shirt and pulled gently. I stepped forward, sifting my fingers into her soft locks.

"I want to make love in our bed. One last time. I want to feel you... Only you. Not all this *hurt*."

I parted my lips to tell her we didn't have time. She stole the words when she went for the button on my jeans and pushed them down. Palming my hardening cock, she dropped to her knees. I closed my eyes with a sigh when her lips came around me. I was certain that death could be knocking on our door, and I'd find a way to justify having her mouth on me just a minute more.

She moaned, and I felt the vibration all the way to my toes. Her tongue twirled and teased the tip, and I swore I couldn't breathe until she took me fully in her mouth again. Then she did, and it was pure goddamn heaven.

"That's it, baby. Take all of me."

She slid her palms over the rough hair on my thighs as I gazed down at her. So much love, so much trust in those big, round eyes. Her strokes went from slow and shallow to fast and deep. The back of her throat massaged my head over and over, sending a jolt of delirious pleasure through my body each time. My abs tightened, and I felt a familiar twinge at the base of my spine.

"Oh, fuck. Kate," I gasped. It was too good, too intense. I wouldn't have a chance to make love to her at this rate.

Against every male instinct I possessed, I withdrew from her mouth and hauled her to her feet. Pushing her back onto the bed, I unfastened her jeans. Pulling the garment down hastily, I freed one leg. Before I could strip her the rest of the way, she sat up, cupped the nape of my neck, and kissed me fiercely, twirling her tongue against mine the way she had my cock seconds ago.

I couldn't wait anymore. I took the space between her legs, ripped her panties to one side and plunged into her. A ragged cry left her lips as I filled her, both of us half naked.

The peace that washed across her features in that moment was one I recognized. The kind of peace that only being with her—inside her, possessing her, loving her—could bring me. A tear leaked from the corner of her eye. I bent and claimed it with my lips, reminding her how much I loved her again and again as our bodies came together.

"This is the only place I ever want to be, Kate. With you, inside you," I whispered against her ear as I thrust deeply. "This is my home."

"I know," she whimpered.

More tears came, mingling with her cries of pleasure. I owned her pain as much as her pleasure now. This was us. I had to accept both.

This place hadn't made us who we were. Our love had. Our vows. Our refusal to let each other go despite impossible circumstances. Whatever chemistry existed between two people who needed each other to survive, that same energy channeled through me and into her, binding us, electrifying every movement.

Her peace had been replaced with rapture. She was there...so close. And hell, so was I. I felt her tense around my cock, adding dizzying friction to every thrust. I was a goddamn slave to her body.

"Come for me, Kate. I want to feel you shatter around me."

She blinked up at me, her lips pink and swollen from our kisses. "I don't want it to end."

I shook my head slightly. "It won't. I promise you, baby. You and me, we're never going to end. Come for me. Feel me."

I banded an arm around her waist and lifted her hips against me. The new angle allowed my cock to drag over her G-spot with every thrust. She clawed at my pectorals with one hand, gripped my hair with the other, and tightened her thighs around my hips.

"I feel you... Price, my God. Ahh!"

She shook like she'd been shattered into a thousand pieces. My climax detonated in time with hers. In that moment, I was everywhere—all around her, inside her, collecting her shattered pieces so I could bring us back together, whole again, where everything was right. If only for a moment.

I struggled to catch my breath and regain control of my brain. I didn't want to rush reality back in so soon, though, so I stayed nestled inside of Kate, savoring the little aftershocks. I breathed her in, tasted the salt on her skin. I sighed heavily before lifting off her. She lay limp on the bed, face flushed, skin slick, with one pant leg still hanging on and her panties a ripped, wet mess.

I bit my lip, because the sight was making me hard again already. I didn't want to stop. Fuck, I wasn't going to either. Stripping her jeans and panties off completely, I tugged her toward the edge of the bed. She widened her eyes but didn't argue when I spread her knees wide and sank my fingers into her soaked pussy.

My release was still warm and slick inside her, easing my strokes. Few things were as satisfying as coming inside her. One day we'd do it with so much more purpose. I was determined to make good on that promise. If we couldn't have a family, I'd have failed her.

"I'm going to give you a baby one day."

She smiled weakly. "I know."

I couldn't decode her expression. Didn't know if it was sadness or faith or regret, or maybe she was too wiped out from her earlier orgasm to give the reaction much force. Uneasy with my inability to read her as easily as I normally could, I deepened my penetration. She closed her eyes and arched into my touch. I was going to make her scream again. And then I was going to fuck her until I forgot what a mess we were in.

◆ ◆ ◆ ◆

After a shower and another few mouthfuls of The Kaphi House's delicious bread, Kate packed two bags—a hiking backpack that we'd used on a few summer trips to the White Mountains, and the carry-on she'd traveled with to Leiloa. I studied her carefully, noting how she paused between the two bags before placing something. I could hear her silent choices. One bag held the essentials, the other held everything else. Everything else that could be left behind if need be. The process took twenty-six minutes.

We left the apartment without a word. No goodbye. No tears. Kate simply locked the door, and we made our way down to the street. I paused at the doorway, peering through the window before pulling my hat—an old ball cap I'd found in the closet—down on my forehead. With sunglasses, it wouldn't render me unrecognizable, but it would obscure my face if anyone was looking for it. Kate had done the same, tucking her long blond hair into a twist under a much more stylish fedora.

We left the building, and Kate took the first steps toward the subway station.

"Wait. Give me one second." I jogged across to the street, stopping in front of a pile of dirty gray blankets and newspaper.

The homeless man I'd spotted through the window earlier looked up at me with a toothless grin. His eyes and smile were exceptionally bright, an unexpected contrast against the materials that surrounded him.

"How can I help you, son?"

"I was wondering if you'd seen anything unusual around here the past couple days."

He pursed his lips, the expression almost cartoonish in the way it deepened the grooves on his thin face. "Unusual?"

"Like anyone coming around that may have seemed suspicious."

He tilted his head back and forth, like he was contemplating. I had a stronger feeling that he was holding out on me. I lowered to my haunches and took out my wallet.

"How much?"

He let out a loud cackle and patted his knee. "How about I tell you, and you give me what you think it's worth?"

I hesitated a moment and then folded my wallet again. "Okay. We'll do it your way."

"My name's Joseph, by the way."

I took his outstretched hand and shook it firmly. "It's good to meet you, Joseph."

"And you are?" He lifted an eyebrow and his crooked smile was back.

"I'm looking for information, Joseph. Can you help me?"

He waved his hand and looked upward. "Sometimes people are so busy looking at the ground, they never look up at the sky."

I followed his gaze. Nothing but gray sky and the uneven lines of brownstone rooftops above us.

"What does that mean?"

He pointed up, past my shoulder. "Right up there on the fourth floor is where I saw them first a couple weeks ago. No one ever seems to look that high. I was on the other side of the street. Café opens up early, and I like the smell of it." He inhaled deeply like he was reliving that first inhale of coffee in the morning.

I empathized, but right now I was more inclined to shake him violently for the information he was spoon-feeding me. "Who, Joseph? What did you see?"

He lifted his chin toward Kate on the other side of the street. "She's pretty. Gets me coffee sometimes, so I notice when she comes and goes. I noticed every time she walked by, they'd be by the window. Then they'd disappear and show up again, speeding by me like they had someplace to go all of a sudden. Couple guys. Tall. Hair so blond it could be white. They've been watching her. I couldn't tell you why, though."

My heart was speeding. My adrenaline kicked up full force. I opened my wallet and threw a few hundred dollars in Joseph's lap. "Did they see me? I got here a couple days ago."

Joseph smiled broadly again. "I'll let you know in a few minutes. Soon as you two mosey down the street, they'll either be right behind you, or they won't."

Fuck.

I didn't thank him. Didn't throw more money his way though he likely deserved it. I raced across the street, grabbed Kate's arm. "We need to go. *Now.*"

CHAPTER FIFTEEN

Kate

I didn't have the first clue why Price had stopped to talk to Old Joe. He was the one who'd been in a rush to leave, but he'd stopped to give a few precious minutes to a stranger? I once knew my husband better than anyone. Now? He was, in many ways, the stranger.

"What were you talking to Old Joe for?"

"He said his name was Joseph."

"It is. Nina and I call him Old Joe. She gives him free coffee, and I take it to him when I'm around. Sometimes I spring for some bread or a scone. He's an alcoholic, but a decent guy. Always has a kind word for me."

"Would you say he's trustworthy?"

I cocked my head. "Why would you ask me that?"

Price looked in every direction and then grabbed my arm and started walking. "Let's not talk here. I'll explain when we get to the hotel."

◆ ◆ ◆ ◆

Price spared no expense getting the best penthouse suite for us, complete with an armed security guard. I hadn't known such a thing existed at a Midtown hotel. Money talked, apparently.

As soon as we were situated, he turned to me. "Have you noticed anyone around the apartment building lately? Anyone when you went out?"

"You mean before I went to Leiloa? No."

"Are you sure?"

"Of course I'm sure. But Price, I wasn't really looking. Remember, I've been existing in a fog for the past year."

He took my hand and led me to the black and green brocade sofa in the living area of our suite. He gently pushed me down and then sat beside me. "I need you to think hard, Kate. Anything? Did anything seem out of place? Any*one*?"

I chewed on my lower lip. "I truly didn't notice."

"What about when you took coffee to Joseph? Did you notice anyone hanging around during those times?"

I shook my head.

"Anyone with, say, really light-blond hair?"

Again I shook my head.

"So blond it could be white?"

"Like platinum blond? No."

Price let out a breath.

"You asked me if Joe was trustworthy. What did he tell you?"

"He said several weeks ago he noticed two blond men hanging around the fourth floor of the building across the street. Every time you left our building, they'd follow you."

A chill hit the back of my neck. "I never went anywhere, Price, except to the coffee shop and the market. Besides the two-week trip to Spain, that is, and last week when I went to the island."

"Damn. If they'd laid a hand on you..." Price stood and began pacing the floor, raking his hands through his hair.

I wanted to stand, to go to my husband and comfort him, assure him I was unharmed. No one had hurt me. But something kept me rooted on that sofa.

Had I been in danger?

If Joe thought someone might pose a threat to me, wouldn't he have let me know? He'd always seemed like such a nice man, a person who'd just had a lot of tough breaks, lost everything, and turned to alcohol. Then again, we'd never really talked. I didn't know his story. Maybe he didn't care about anything except his next drink.

Price walked back toward me. "Kate, please. Think hard."

"If I had seen guys with platinum-blond hair, I would remember."

"You would? Because this is New York, Kate. I saw a guy with green hair on the subway. Light blond doesn't seem so out of place."

"I wish I could help you. It's possible I did see them and didn't notice."

"Well, they saw you."

"According to Joe. Who, while he's a nice guy, could have made the whole thing up to make a buck."

"He gave me the information before I paid him," Price said.

"So what? You want to know why Nina gives him coffee every day? To sober him up. He's a drunk, Price. Aaryan and Nina have tried to help him. They offered him a job, but he said no."

"He wasn't drunk when I talked to him."

"Maybe not. I have no idea." I grabbed his arm and pulled him down next to me. "There's nothing we can do about that now. Tell the hired gun outside to be on the watch for the blond guys, and in the meantime, let's take a look at your files."

He nodded, his lips a thin line. After speaking to the guard, he grabbed his laptop, set it up at the desk, and pulled another chair over from the table. I sat down next to him. He inserted the thumb drive.

"There might be some stuff in here you don't understand," he said.

I couldn't help a laugh. "I'm a journalist. I have to become an expert in anything I report on. I'll figure it out."

"God." He closed his eyes for a moment. "That was so fucking patronizing. I'm sorry, baby. You're the smartest person I know. Of course you'll figure it out."

I caressed his muscular forearm. "Let's take a look. Together."

Price opened a file. "I didn't keep any of my own research on here, just the quarterly reports and stock analysis. I didn't want to take the chance of anyone finding this file and figuring out I was watching the company. Everything else was encrypted on my other laptop, which went down with the plane."

"You didn't back it up?"

"I did, but I don't know if I can get to it."

"Where is it?"

"At my parents' house. I wanted it somewhere safe."

I sighed. "All right. Explain to me what's going on."

"I started watching Cybermark Enterprises a couple years ago. They'd gone public about two years previously, and they were a unicorn."

"A unicorn?"

"A new company that is valued at over a billion dollars."

I sucked in a breath. "Wow. How does a brand new company get that kind of money?"

"Lots of ways. They could have been private for many years and built up business. They could have gotten an influx of cash from an inheritance or an investor. Or a host of other ways. It can be perfectly legal, but it's uncommon, so when I saw this unicorn I kept my eye on it."

"Did they get the money illegally?"

"It's possible they set it up as a Ponzi scheme, but they covered their tracks. I wasn't able to find any solid proof. No one knows where the money came from originally, though I have a theory."

"So what happened? What made you start to ask questions?"

"Things went fine for about six months or so. I didn't make any trades yet because I wasn't quite comfortable with the unicorn concept, but I always tracked the company. The stock was performing well, and according to my system, should have kept going up. But the price started to stagnate."

"Why?"

"That's what I wanted to know. And that's where this all begins."

My nerves jumped throughout my body. I was about to learn the truth that had taken my husband from me.

The truth, whether I was ready for it or not.

"I started doing some research into the inner workings and personnel. Turned out they'd had some turnover in their accounting department right around the time the stock started stagnating. The week after I began my research, they fired their CFO and hired a new one."

"Cleaning house isn't necessarily a bad thing. I mean, if their stock was going down, maybe they needed some fresh insight."

"Maybe. It's possible. But not likely. You see, Kate, the stock price has little to do with how the company is actually doing. It's all about the market."

"Okay..."

"The replacement of the CFO made the *Wall Street Journal*, so it was common knowledge. What wasn't common knowledge was that the entire accounting department turned over along with the CFO. I found this out when I dug deeper. The stock shifted down a little, which is normal. A change in personnel always jars the market a little."

"Makes sense."

"The stock went back up within a few days, but was still undervalued according to my system. Anyway, I kept watching, and within another month, they replaced the CFO again."

"Again?"

"Yes. So this made the third CFO in about six months. Again, it made the news. The entire department turned over again, but this time I didn't have to dig for the information. The Director of Corporate Relations made the news public, citing his desire for transparency. Only hours later, allegations of accounting irregularities popped up, and this time, the stock price bottomed out."

"Because investors panicked."

"Exactly. This was bad business, especially for a company supposedly worth a billion dollars. So I got even more nosy. And you know what they say. Curiosity killed the cat."

I swatted him. "That's not even slightly funny. And you're not dead, thank God."

"I began asking questions. A lot of questions. Found out the company wanted to reacquire a majority of its shares."

"Why would they want to do that?"

"There could be many reasons. It's not that uncommon of an occurrence. It could have been as simple as them wanting to consolidate ownership. But it caught my eye again, because corporate buybacks for a startup company are unusual. Most startups are focused on top-line growth, not reacquisition of stock. For whatever reason, though, they were set on reacquiring shares, so they invented the accounting turmoil to drive the stock price down. Once it hit bottom, they could buy up the shares they wanted."

"Did they do it?"

"They did. After they thought I was dead."

"I'm not following. Why did they want you dead?"

"They were deliberately manipulating the market so their stock value would go down and they could buy it up when it hit rock bottom. That's illegal in the US and in most other countries as well. They found out I was doing a lot of digging. At that point, though, I had no proof. Only a hunch. I never in a million years thought they'd want me dead for it. You have to know, Kate, that I'd never have deliberately put myself in danger. I'd never have gotten on that plane if I'd thought..." He rubbed his forehead. "God..."

I kissed his cheek. "I know that, babe."

He sighed. "You don't know how many times I've relived this. Wished I'd just let sleeping dogs lie."

"That's not who you are. It's not who I am either."

"I know." He sighed again.

"Did you ever get proof? I mean, that the turnover wasn't just... turnover?"

"I did. I came into some information."

"Go on."

"I met a guy who did some contract work for a company they hired to test their security system. He inadvertently uncovered some files proving it was all a scam to drive the stock price down."

"God, Price. Out of all the people on the planet, how did you happen to find this particular guy?"

He smiled. "He found me. It was Otis."

I nearly fell off my chair. "Otis?"

"Yeah. How do you think I found Leiloa? I found Otis first."

"He's just a kid."

"He's twenty-one, and a genius. He was contracting for a little company in the South Pacific, and Cybermark hired them to test their security. It makes perfect sense. They wouldn't use some big corporate security firm. They'd find some obscure little guy who they could pay to keep quiet."

"But Otis didn't keep quiet."

"Oh, he did. But he's kind of like me. Curious. After my computer went down with the plane, I couldn't contact my parents to get my backup files, so I had to begin again. Otis ended up finding me through my IP signature from my research."

"He hacked you?"

Price smiled. "Yeah. He did. Good thing, too, because I wouldn't have survived this past year without him."

"Why didn't you go to the authorities?"

"We can't, Kate. Otis could go to prison."

"Did he hack the system on purpose?"

"No. It was incidental to what he was hired to do."

"Then what's the problem?"

"The problem is, Kate, that their goons would fucking murder us before we could make a deal with the Feds. He and I have talked through this a million times, and it's a no-win. We've managed to keep Otis's identity a secret so far, and he doesn't want to go to the authorities."

I widened my eyes. "Is Otis even his real name?"

He shook his head. "I don't know. I never told him my real name, not until the end."

"Wow." I let out a breath. "Just wow. I can't believe this."

"Believe it, and it gets worse."

"Oh God." I clutched at my stomach, feeling suddenly nauseated. "What else?"

"Otis kept digging. We found out some of these people aren't just white-collar criminals. They're into some nasty shit."

"Oh God," I said again. "Do I want to know?"

"The major shareholder of Cybermark is a man named Kelly Maguire."

"And?"

"He's a drug kingpin, Kate. Meth trade. And the Director of Corporate Relations, who was leaking the turnover news, is his lackey. His mouthpiece."

My stomach threatened to empty as Price continued.

"And they don't abide by anyone's rules."

Drugs? How did my sweet husband manage to get involved in this? All for some curiosity about a stock that wasn't performing according to his system?

"How is this possible? How can you know this? Why hasn't he been caught?"

"Because he's clean, Kate. He owns the shares through a bunch of offshore holding companies, and he's manipulating the stock price in the short term for a gain in the long term. His name isn't associated with Cybermark in any way. I dug too deep. I'm onto them, and they know it."

I stood, clutching at my stomach. "You said you had a theory about where the money for the startup came from. It's drug money, isn't it?"

"I honestly don't know, baby, but that's my guess, yes. The company is clean on paper, but it could have been laundered drug money."

Acid rose in my throat, and my vision blurred. Drugs... Danger...

"Kate?" Price stood.

I fell into his arms.

Couldn't see...

Couldn't breathe...

"It's okay. You just need to lie down." He led me into the bedroom and helped me onto the king-size bed.

I was shivering. So cold. I looked into his warm brown eyes.

"Breathe. It's okay, baby. I'm going to take care of you. I'm going to take care of *us*."

I gradually got my breathing under control. All this time I'd wanted the whole story from him, and now...

Fuck. Ignorance had been bliss.

Drugs. Anything went in the drug business. Murder was an everyday occurrence. All in the name of the almighty dollar.

"Kate, baby. Talk to me."

I wrapped my arms around Price's neck and pulled him to me. "Don't want to talk. Kiss me."

He crushed his mouth to mine and I took from him, escaping the utter mess that our lives had become. Need overwhelmed me. I needed Price. Inside me. Now.

I kissed him frantically, nipping at his lips, sucking them into my mouth, twirling my tongue around his. Already my nipples were hardening, my pussy throbbing. I couldn't get there quickly enough. Ached for him to shove his big cock into me and fuck me into oblivion. Suspend reality, if only for a moment.

I lowered one hand and worked at his belt. His cock was hard and ready.

"God, Kate," he said against my chin.

"Now, Price. Please. Now."

He lugged my jeans over my hips, and I shimmied out of them. I'd managed to unbuckle his belt and unzip his pants, and once his cock was free, he plunged inside me with a low groan.

Home. With Price, I was home. After his stunning revelation, I needed to feel the raw part of us, the component that made us uniquely us, the pleasure our bodies could give each other.

Soon he was panting against me, sweat dripping from his brow. "Can't hold on. Need to come, Kate."

With his words, I catapulted into the rapturous abyss with him, and for a few timeless moments we were safe, wrapped in each other's guarded cloaks where nothing could harm us.

CHAPTER SIXTEEN

Price

As Kate slumbered in the hotel bed, I stared out the window. Outside, the city hummed with a steady flow of traffic and pedestrians. We could not be farther from our Leiloa oasis. This was our prison now... until we found a way out of this mess.

Part of me regretted letting Kate bring us back to New York. Her stunned reaction to the information I'd uncovered about Cybermark didn't help. I pinched the bridge of my nose and exhaled heavily. Maybe I should have told her more, given her a clearer picture of who we were dealing with. If I had, perhaps we'd be sipping rum drinks somewhere off the Pacific coast right now. Not running for our lives.

Being at the hotel made me feel marginally better. I had no doubt we were safer here, but I was still edgy and paranoid, ready to fight or flee at the first sign of danger. I knew sleep wouldn't come easily, not until I had a plan. I settled behind the desk and opened my laptop again. I scrolled through my files, willing my brain to think harder and zero in on any details I may have missed.

Think. Think. Think.

The more I perused, the more my doubts grew. I couldn't have been alone in my suspicions of Cybermark, could I? If no one else had uncovered anything suspicious, how would I?

Maybe my single point of view was the problem. If Kate was determined to expose Cybermark, she'd need more than my personal interpretation of what wrongdoing could be going on behind the scenes. Any reporter worth his salt would seek additional sources to fill in the gaps. Gaps that I'd failed to fill on my information-seeking mission in Zurich. Gaps I wasn't willing to fill with findings that could threaten Otis's freedom.

Slowly an idea began to form. I pulled up the articles related to the accounting department turnovers. I grabbed a pen and scratched the names of the ex-employees on the hotel stationery. If they knew anything incriminating, they'd likely never talk let alone risk their lives as I had. But it was a place to start.

Quickly I typed the first person's name into my search bar. *Victoria Williamson.* I scanned the results. A profile on a business social network showed she still worked at Cybermark. Odd. I dug deeper and found her Facebook account, which appeared to have been abandoned. Nothing had been posted for over a year. My next hit was an obituary. For one hopeful moment, I assured myself that she simply shared a name with someone much older who'd passed on.

But no. Victoria Williamson had died in a tragic skiing accident in Chamonix, a resort nestled in the French Alps. Dread took root as I scratched a line through her name and searched for the next person on the list.

Marc LeBaron. The search returned an article as the first

result. "Former Finance Executive Found Dead in Greenwood Lake."

The meager contents of my stomach threatened to rise when I clicked the article. He'd died in what was believed to be a freak accident, having fallen from his boat during an early morning fishing trip. With a shaky hand, I scratched his name out and searched the next person on the list.

"Price?"

Kate's voice, raspy from sleep, pulled my focus from the laptop screen. She sat up with a frown, covering her nakedness with the sheet. "Is everything okay?"

Was everything okay? I couldn't begin to answer that question. Instead, I turned back to the screen and continued the search, driven by the suddenly desperate need to find someone alive on it.

They couldn't have... But they could.

They'd already proven they could eliminate a person, or at least try to, like the cold-blooded killers they were.

Kate's voice hovered in the background, but my unnerving train of thought drowned her out.

Trey Otto. Three clicks. Accidental overdose.

Marcia Breininger. Two clicks. Car accident.

"Price!"

I jolted hard at the loud sound combined with Kate's hand on my shoulder, shaking me.

"Price, will you talk to me?"

I caught her hand, held it firmly between us. Only then did I realize I was uncomfortably warm. My palms were moist and my breaths came hard and fast.

"They're all dead."

Her eyes became two round saucers. "What? Who?"

I shook my head quickly. "No, it's okay. Well, not really. Those people I told you were fired from Cybermark. I'm not even done with the list. I just can't believe it. How could they get away with it?"

She squeezed my hand tightly. "Price, goddamnit. Slow down. You're not making any sense."

I took a deep breath and tried to organize my thoughts. "I realized we should try to reach out to someone who was with the company. See if anyone would be willing to talk, or at least point us in the right direction. So far, every one of the people I've searched for who left their accounting team is dead. Freak accidents. Every one of them."

She simply stared at me for a few seconds before glancing down at the list I'd systematically scratched out. She lifted the piece of paper and studied it a moment before turning away. She plunked down on the sofa with her own laptop, referring to the paper once more before typing furiously on the keys.

I stood and went to her. "I've spent the past twenty minutes going through that list. Don't you believe me?"

"I'm not questioning you. I just want to see for myself."

I shoved my hands through my hair and paced the floor in front of her. Retracing my actions would prove a gruesome journey. The sick feeling had only deepened with each new discovery. Being outside the company, my name would have never been on that list, but I could have shared their fates. Instead I was here. Living, breathing, and very likely one of the only people who was connecting the dots. Cybermark was in the business of data mining, scamming millions, and outright murdering anyone who got in their path.

Suddenly the prospect of running away from all this seemed impossible. Beyond impossible. *Wrong.* The very word Kate had used to describe it when we were back on the island.

"We have to dig deeper," I said suddenly. "I made that list from articles that had come out months before the crash. I hadn't bothered keeping track of Cybermark's activity much after that, but there have to be others." An idea shot like a bolt to the front of my thoughts. I rushed to my laptop. "What's the date on Victoria Williamson's obit?"

"November. Five months after you disappeared."

I found the date on the article noting her departure from the company. "She left in January of that year. So they waited almost a year. What about Marc LeBaron?"

"July. He had a summer home on the lake."

"They fired him in March. He'd returned to the States, so maybe that gave them a sense of urgency. Hell, who knows. But this at least means that we can look for any recent departures from the accounting department and try to get to them before they do."

Kate's stare was fixed on the screen as mine had been earlier.

"Kate, do you hear me? We need to make that list and track down whoever we can. Between the unusual numbers I noticed long ago and any tips someone might be able to give us, I think we could break this wide open. You were right to want to take this to the press. There's so much more to expose than I ever would have imagined. And once people see that ex-Cybermark employees are dropping like flies, it could be just enough to keep us protected."

She looked up. "I think I know who to go to first."

"Who?"

She chewed at her bottom lip. "You're not going to like it."

"Are you kidding me? We could be looking at a death toll of a dozen or more. Why the hell would I care who we give the scoop to as long as they're reputable?"

"Alejandro emailed me this morning."

I stopped pacing and faced her. "Alejandro? As in—"

"As in the journalist I met in Spain. He recently moved to New York and got a job with the *Journal*. He said he wants to reconnect."

I balled my fists. I relished the thought of connecting one of them to his face. "No. We'll find someone else."

She slapped her hands on the cushions on either side of her. "Why? It could take days or weeks for me to get someone else to give us time. I could meet with him right away. If we already have people tailing us, we may not have a lot of time to tap resources here in the city before it gets too dangerous. Hell, it already is too dangerous."

My next thought was a terrible one. I'd never wished for anyone to get caught up in this mess. Someone else knowing the things I knew guaranteed a path fraught with peril. But if we sent anyone on this journey to dig deeper into Cybermark's many wrongdoings, perhaps Alejandro would be the perfect candidate.

How could I hate a man I'd never met? I wasn't sure, but knowing he'd had his hands and mouth on my wife singed my already frayed nerves.

"Fine." I bit the word out.

Kate lifted her eyebrows. "Fine?"

"We'll meet with him."

"We? You're still dead, remember?"

I winced and began pacing again. Kate was right. She could deliver all the pertinent information without revealing that I was still alive. That also meant she'd appear single and available for his advances again. If he touched her...

I stopped abruptly. "I'll go with you. You can meet him in a public place. Someplace busy enough to give you anonymity and so I can stay close without him noticing."

She nodded. "That should work."

I couldn't believe I was agreeing to this. Then again, I was still grappling with the new information I'd just discovered. What choice did I have? I was in New York, about to see the man who'd tried to fuck my wife, so he could write a story that could save both of us from a life on the run. How had this become my life? Didn't matter. I didn't have time or the mental wherewithal to make sense of it all.

"Email him and set up a time. I'll make a copy of my files and see who else I can put on this list. Hopefully someone without an obituary."

"Got it."

◆ ◆ ◆ ◆

Kate fussed with her hair. I braced my hands on either side of the doorway, studying everything. Her undeniable beauty. Her nervous hands. The faraway look in her eyes, like her thoughts had already taken her into the future. In less than an hour, she'd be face to face with Alejandro. She tugged at the bottom of her sweater and canted her head.

"You look beautiful. I'm sure he'll agree."

She found my gaze in the mirror, her shoulders softening.

"Price, don't be like that."

I exhaled slowly. "I'm not upset with you. I just don't like this guy."

She sighed and stared at her reflection a moment. "I know. It's occurred to me that the better I look for this meeting, the more likely he may be to help me. But of course everything about that feels wrong."

I came behind her, holding her back against my front. "You're just being smart and calculating how to get what you want. You're using all the tools at your disposal to survive. Trust me, I know how it feels."

"This won't be anything like what you've endured, Price."

"No. But it's still risky for you. It's still outside your comfort zone. And you're pushing through it against all your instincts."

She closed her eyes a moment and then turned in my embrace. Resting her hands on my chest, she flicked her gaze up. "Speaking of instincts, I need to tell you something. Something else you're not going to like."

I held my breath and studied her, finding no clues in her clear blue eyes. "Tell me."

"That night I had dinner with Alejandro. I told you he'd kissed me."

In an instant my body became a block of rigid muscle. Good God. What if she'd slept with him? What if she'd spared my feelings once but couldn't hold up the lie once she was in the same room with him?

She tried to step back, but I wouldn't budge. "Kate, what is it? Tell me now."

"He was...aggressive with me."

I grimaced. "Aggressive how?"

"When I rejected him gently the first time, it was like he didn't believe me. He kept on, like if he kissed and groped me enough, I'd get turned on and sleep with him. Obviously it didn't work. I had to get aggressive back for him to get the message that I wasn't interested."

My thoughts spun in angry circles. I wanted to kill him. Having Kate meet with him had been a terrible idea. But putting him in harm's way to save our future wasn't. Did Alejandro groping my wife warrant a possible death sentence?

"It's like I can read your thoughts," she said, her tone filled with worry.

"What am I thinking?"

"That you want to kill him and that this was all a terrible idea."

I pressed my lips into a flat line. "Pretty much spot on."

"We need this, Price. Giving the *Journal* the scoop is too important. We can't get sidetracked worrying about whatever base male thoughts Alejandro might be having about me in the process. I told you because I didn't want you to get caught off guard if he was more forward than you expected. Last thing I need is for you to fly off the handle in the middle of my meeting with him, exposing that you're alive and killing any possibility of getting him to work with us."

"Then it's good you told me, because if he touches you, that's exactly what I'll want to do." Everything she said made sense in my head. None of it eased my intense urge to destroy the man who didn't want to take "no" for an answer.

"I'll be fine. Penn Station isn't exactly an intimate meeting place. I'll talk to him, give him the facts, and if he wants a second meeting with his editor, we'll set it up and go from there."

The new knot in my stomach wouldn't go away. I knew this is what we had to do, but suddenly everything about it felt wrong. Of course, nothing about our current predicament felt right. I simply had to push through this discomfort to get us closer to the truth. And hopefully the truth would set us free—free to live the life we deserved.

Without releasing her, I checked my watch. It was four thirty. The subway would be mobbed the closer we got to five.

"We should go."

When I began to step away, Kate brought her hands to my face, keeping us close. She stared into my eyes for a moment, like she was trying to communicate without words. A feeling maybe, or something so profound she simply couldn't speak it.

"What is it, baby?"

"I love you, Price," she whispered. "My love for you never once lessened simply because you were gone. It only grew. Every day it grew, because I had nothing but time to remember what we had together. Everything I took for granted. All the little things. A thousand little stabs of memory compounded onto the crazy love I'd had for you before that day. Nothing and no one will ever be able to take that away. You could still be gone, and I would still be yours in my heart. So completely yours. I need you to know that."

I didn't have any words because she'd said them all. When I kissed her, our mouths came together softly at first, and then hungrily. The physical connection became the channel for all my passion and devotion, pouring from me into her. Kate. The love of my life. My wife.

I hoisted her onto the counter, dragging my lips down her neck. Kissing, sucking, biting. I pressed her thighs wide and teased my thumb along the seam of her jeans, adding just enough pressure to make her moan.

Fuck. We didn't have time for this, but I couldn't stop. I went for the button on her jeans and tugged, but she caught my hand.

"We can't."

"I need to be inside you, Kate."

"I want you too, but we need to go." Desire and reason mingled in her plea.

I growled, hating that she was right. I took a few breaths and tried to get my wits about me again. Slowly I stepped back, giving her enough room to scoot off the counter and pass into the bedroom for her jacket and purse.

I followed her out. I could do this. I could keep my shit together, watching her with Alejandro. If I could live without Kate for a year, I could endure a few more minutes without her in my arms, knowing another man wanted what was mine.

◆ ◆ ◆ ◆

Penn Station was as busy as we'd expected. The train terminal was teeming with commuters, tourists, and seemingly every walk of life. How she'd spot Alejandro amidst the chaos, I wasn't sure. I hadn't had the time to research him and regretted it immediately after she'd told me about their encounter. The curiosity was eating at me almost as much as my fierce jealousy.

I hung back on the other side of the terminal, my ball cap pulled down low, shadowing my eyes.

I saw the recognition in her expression before I saw the man himself. He was tall. Dark-haired with olive skin. And because in that moment I was measuring the ways she could have been attracted to him, I admitted that he wasn't a terrible-looking human being. Tall, dark, and handsome. He smiled as he approached. Straight white teeth seemed to beam against his skin. He came in for a hug, which she returned. I had expected that. Didn't keep me from seeing red, but I was ready for it.

They exchanged niceties. I could tell from her body language and soft smile. Then her expression smoothed. As she began speaking, I knew she was beginning to tell him about the story. She gestured with her hands, like she was outlining all the points we'd discussed earlier. I shifted my focus to him, expecting to see intrigue, admiration, even latent desire. I saw none of it. What I saw was worse. A blank, cold expression void of anything that spoke to his willingness to help her...*us*. He glanced over his shoulder and then reached out to touch hers, stopping whatever she was saying. I couldn't make out the words from reading his lips, but he motioned behind him. She shot a look my way, but before I could signal her to stay put, she followed him deeper into the growing crowd.

I took long strides in her direction, no longer concerned about hanging back and staying inconspicuous. But they turned a corner and she slipped out of sight. Where was he taking her? The closest exit was the other way. Around the corner, I scanned heads for Kate's blond hair. Every second I couldn't see her was a second I couldn't breathe. Where the fuck did she go?

I pushed through the crowd. Looked up and down. Seconds

felt like minutes. Every blonde was Kate until I realized she wasn't, sending my heart flying and crashing against my ribs. Panic wrapped around me like a second skin.

"Kate!" I looked in every direction and screamed her name. I didn't care who saw me now. "Alejandro!"

But she was gone. I'd lost her.

CHAPTER SEVENTEEN

Kate

My heart pounded as I chased Alejandro through the throng of people.

If you want to save your husband, follow me.

His words played over and over again in my ears, as if they were on constant rewind. I hurried to keep up with him. When he looked over his shoulder at me, his expression vague, he grabbed my hand and forced me along with him.

"Alejandro!" I yelled. "Stop! I can't keep up."

Still he towed me through the herd of passersby. I mumbled "excuse me" several times when I accidently knocked into someone. My arms would no doubt be bruised when this was over.

Alejandro was different. He'd been charming and full of personality on our date—until he'd gotten forceful at the end. He was still forceful today, but where was the charm? I'd tried to ask questions before following him, but he hadn't answered. I'd had no choice but to go. I'd do anything to save Price. Besides, Alejandro was a journalist, like I was. He was interested in the truth.

I looked over my shoulder, searching for Price's baseball cap. I didn't see him, but he'd be tailing me. I knew him too well. He'd never abandon me. However, if he was truly in danger, I hoped he'd lose me. I couldn't bear the thought—

Thud!

I crashed into Alejandro's back. *That's what you get for not watching where you're going, Kate.* It didn't faze him. He kept tugging me along, until finally the crowd of people began to disperse. He pulled me out a double door and onto the street. I was disoriented. Before I could assess our whereabouts, Alejandro pushed me into a waiting limousine and got in next to me.

"Hello, Kate."

I startled and turned toward the voice. On my other side sat a man—a man with platinum-blond hair.

"Wh-Who are you?"

"My name is Sven."

"You... You're the one Old Joe talked about. But he said there were two of you."

"My twin brother, Krister. He's taking care of...other things at the moment. We've been watching you, Kate."

My blood ran cold and my hackles rose. I turned to Alejandro next to me. "We need to go. These people aren't who you think they are." I reached across Alejandro to the door handle.

He stopped me, a soft chuckle escaping his throat. "Sven and I are old friends, Catalina." He placed his hand on my knee.

I whisked his hand away. "Don't you dare touch me," I said through clenched teeth. "You're one of them? What about our time in Spain?"

"I was digging. Trying to get information on your husband."

"I thought he was dead."

"Yes, that became clear fairly quickly."

The night in Spain came back to me like an IMAX movie. Alejandro grabbing my hair, squeezing my breast...

Please, Catalina. I know you want me as much as I want you. Let me take you to bed.

My throat constricted and my stomach clenched. Once he realized he couldn't get any information out of me, he'd decided to try to get a fuck instead. *Bastard.*

I swallowed and looked back to Sven. His hair was indeed nearly white, as were his eyebrows. So odd. How could I have not seen him and his brother lurking around?

Simple. I hadn't been looking. I'd been awash in my own heartbreak. The same reason I hadn't seen Alejandro for who he was. Because I'd been grieving Price.

Price. God, where was Price?

Then it hit me. "Your brother is taking care of other things, you said. What other things?"

Sven's lips twitched into a half smile. "He's delivering a message."

"To whom?" I demanded.

"You're a smart lady, Catalina," Alejandro said. "You already know."

I brought my fist down hard on Alejandro's thigh. "You think you can get your hands on Price? He's avoided you and the other assholes this far. He'll get away again."

"No, he won't, love," Sven said in his deep growling voice. "Because this time we have a bargaining chip."

I gulped. *Me.* Price would do anything to keep me safe.

I didn't believe in any kind of psychic bullshit, but I closed my eyes and conjured my husband in my mind. He and I were soul mates. Maybe I could reach him.

Don't come after me, my love. Please. I'll find a way back to you somehow. If you come after me, you'll be in danger. Stay put.

I opened my eyes, berating myself for taking my eyes off my surroundings. I needed to figure out where we were going. I looked beyond Sven, but he'd drawn shades over the windows. I frantically began tapping on the black barrier separating us from the driver. "Hey! Hey! They're kidnapping me. Help!"

"Quiet down, Catalina. He's not going to help you."

"Because he's working with you guys. I know that. But if you think I'm not going to try anything I can to get out of here, you can—"

Thonk!

My head hit the back of the seat. I gasped as the sting permeated my flesh. Alejandro had hit me.

"Listen, *puta,*" he said. "Do as we tell you, or things will get ugly. Don't forget our night in Spain. I could have had you then if I'd wanted you. Don't make the mistake of thinking it was *your* decision that we didn't fuck that night."

I turned to him. The sting in my cheek was now a dull ache. "You told me you were a journalist. I should have known better."

"I *was* a journalist once. Doesn't pay the bills as well as I'd like."

So you sold out. I didn't say it. I didn't want to get punched again. Not that I feared a good beating, but I needed to stay conscious if I was going to figure a way out of this.

Sven put a cell phone to his ear. "Let's go," he said.

I looked around for something I might be able to use as a

weapon, or as...anything. Alejandro had taken my purse and set it on the floor by his feet. Maybe I could grab it.

"Why aren't we moving?" Alejandro asked.

"Must be traffic." Sven put the phone to his ear again. "I said, 'let's go.'"

A few seconds passed.

"Dodge? You there?" Sven threw the phone to the floor of the limo and banged on the barrier. "Dodge? Let's go, damn it!"

Still nothing.

"For Christ's sake." Sven opened the door on his side.

He was gone less than a minute before I heard, "Fuck!"

Sven stuck his head back in the door. "Take her, and let's get out of here."

"What's going on?" Alejandro demanded.

"Dodge is dead. Shot in the head. We need to move. Now!"

Without thinking, I scrambled out of the seat and barreled right into Sven, knocking him down.

"Bitch!" he yelled.

People were everywhere, thank God. Crowds meant safety. They wouldn't dare take me screaming and yelling. As much as I wanted to grab the first person I saw and scream for help, I knew that would do no good. I'd just be dragging another innocent soul into this horror. I had to get lost in the crowd. Quickly.

"Kate!"

Alejandro's voice. He was close, so I began sprinting back toward Penn Station. Back to Price.

If he was still there...

No. Couldn't go there. Price was too smart to get caught. He'd eluded them so far.

But now he thought they had me...

My stomach twisted into knots.

"Goddamnit, no!" I said aloud. We had not come this far to lose each other again. I would find Price, or I would die trying.

I resisted the urge to head back into the station. Though I could easily get lost in the crowd, the chances of finding Price were slim. I hadn't thought to grab my purse. *Damn*! That meant they had my cell. They could call Price, and he'd think they had me because the call would come from my phone.

Policemen were everywhere, and again I resisted my instinct. Until I knew Price was safe, I couldn't go running to the law.

When I had gotten far enough that I thought I had lost Alejandro and Sven, I ducked into an office building.

"May I help you?" the door attendant asked.

"Just need to use your restroom, please."

"Of course. Past the front desk and to the left."

I nodded to the security guard at the desk as I walked swiftly toward the ladies' room and entered. Thank God. No bathroom attendant. I took sanctuary in a stall to think, but my thoughts were jumbled. I had no phone. No laptop. No wallet. No money. What the hell was I supposed to do?

First things first. I needed to contact Price to let him know I was okay, and for that, I'd need a phone. Perhaps there was a public phone nearby, maybe at the front desk. I'd ask the security guard in the lobby.

I left the stall and assessed my appearance in the mirror. My blond hair was in disarray, and my cheek was red and beginning to bruise from Alejandro's blow. Nothing to do about that. I had no makeup. I gathered my courage and left the restroom.

When the security desk came into view—

Shit! The back of a platinum-blond head. I clamped my hand over my mouth. Sven was talking to the security guard.

I turned and fled. I couldn't go back to the restroom. The guard would have told Sven where I'd gone. I looked around quickly, and when a freight elevator in the back of the building opened, I rushed in without thinking, nearly toppling over the people attempting to get out.

"So sorry," I mumbled, and pushed the button for the twenty-fifth floor. Best to get as far away as I could from Sven. If he didn't find me in the bathroom, maybe he'd think I'd gone on my way. Besides, surely I'd find a phone on the twenty-fifth floor somewhere.

I didn't make it to twenty-five. The elevator stopped on five for two men hauling boxes, and I rushed out, my pulse racing. I headed to the first office door I found, an architectural firm. I inhaled a deep breath and walked in.

"Hello," a bright-eyed receptionist said. "May I help you?"

"Yes, please. I'm afraid I've just been—" I'd been about to say "mugged." Not a good idea. She'd insist on calling the cops. "I mean, I seem to have lost my purse. My cell phone was in it, and I need to contact my husband and let him know I'm going to miss our lunch date. Could I use a phone?"

"You lost your purse on the fifth floor? Let me call around. I'm sure we can locate it."

"No, no. I mean..." *Think, Kate. Think.* "I lost it on the subway. Someone must have cut the strap. I didn't realize it was gone until now." God, I sounded like a moron. "Please. I need to use a phone."

The woman looked at me, her brows raised. "Well, all right. There's a phone for clients over there." She pointed to an end table in a seating area.

"Perfect. Thank you so much." I tried not to run to the phone. I sat down slowly in a wingback chair and picked up the receiver, punching in Price's new cell number.

It rang once.

Twice.

Three times.

Why wasn't he answering? Had they gotten to him?

Four times.

Five ti—

"Who is this?"

Warmth surged into me. Price's voice. My husband's voice. He was safe.

"Price," I whispered frantically. "Thank God."

"Kate? Is that you?"

"It's me. Alejandro is in on it. He was with one of the blond guys Old Joe was talking about. They had me in a limo, but the driver got shot."

"Shot?" His voice was low and frantic. "Where are you? Are you okay?"

"I got away, but they know where I am. I don't have my purse or my phone."

"Where are you, baby?" he asked again.

I looked to the receptionist. She had her headphones on and was busy typing. "I'm in an office building near Penn Station. I didn't see the address. I'm on the fifth floor at some architectural company." Why hadn't I memorized the name?

"If they know you're there, you have to leave. Now."

"I know, but I'm stuck on the fifth floor."

"Damn!"

"Price, listen to me. They're after you. There's another blond guy."

"I caught sight of him. I've been avoiding him so far."

Relief swept through me. "Thank God. Are you still at Penn Station?"

"Yeah. But I'm coming to you, baby. I'm coming."

"No!" I looked up to the receptionist again after my harsh, though still whispered, outburst. She was still typing. "I'll come to you. I don't know what building I'm in, but I can get back to the station."

"Kate, please."

"It's the only way, Price. I have to get out of here somehow, or they'll eventually find me. They know I'm here. I saw the other blond guy talking to the security guard in the lobby."

He sighed across the phone—his signal that he knew I was right. "Kate, be careful. Please, baby. I can't lose you."

I blinked back the tears that threatened. I couldn't break down now. "You won't. We've come this far. We have to make it. I love you, Price."

"I love you, Kate. Come back to me."

"I will. I promise." I hung up the phone.

I hadn't yet broken a promise to my husband, and I didn't intend to start now.

I stood, nodded to the receptionist and mouthed "thank you," and then walked out the door. A couple of people bustled in the hallway. I smiled and looked around for a door leading to the stairs to stay out of sight.

No. Not a good idea. Sven would take the stairs, and if he found me there, I'd be trapped. I'd never outrun him, and the stairs would be deserted. No one would be around, and Sven would easily be able to outmaneuver me, especially if Alejandro or anyone else was with him. The freight elevator I'd come up in wouldn't work either, as it would be in less frequent use. I had to stay where people were. People offered me protection. People were also witnesses.

I'd take the main elevator and hope like hell I'd miss Sven. Or if I didn't, that there were others around so he couldn't do anything.

What in the world had Price gotten us into? I rehashed his tale about Cybermark in my mind. I'd been freaked out when he told me, but now that I was in the middle of it, fearing for my life and his, the truth had kicked me in the ass with a combat boot.

This was real.

And we could die.

I walked to the elevators, breathed in deeply, and pushed the down button.

CHAPTER EIGHTEEN

Price

A flash of familiar white-blond hair hung in my periphery. I lowered the phone and turned, expecting to make eye contact with the man I'd noticed was following me on my search for Kate. But he hadn't seen me. A large group of college-aged girls were lingering nearby with their bags. I ducked behind them and settled on my haunches, letting my back rest against the wall. Quickly I pulled up the map application on my phone and searched for architectural firms nearby. If Kate was on the move, I'd try like hell to meet her half way.

"I'm so hungover," said a girl close by.

Another girl groaned. "Oh my God, I know. I thought I was going to throw up in the cab on the way here. That guy was driving like a maniac."

I rolled my eyes. I'd pay for her problems. Laughter and more stories of drunken debauchery ensued as I waited endlessly for the search results to offer Kate's possible location. Service was exceptionally shitty in this building. I cursed it and the gaggle of idiotic girls next to me every second the search wheel spun.

Finally, a hit.

Moniz & Whitehead Architectural Associates was on 34th and 8th. That had to be it. I rose and glanced around for the man who'd been following me. He was nowhere to be seen. Frankly, I didn't care as much about the threat of him as I did about moving swiftly in Kate's direction. I wasn't confident he'd attempt to shoot me in public. Didn't seem to be Cybermark's style, as vicious as they were.

I headed toward the exit that would deposit me on 8th Avenue. Kate was close. Barely a block away. Hundreds of people filled the streets between us, but those people were our protection. I just had to get to her.

"Price Lewis?"

I spun at the sound of a man's voice. Two more men in suits flanked me at once, the air of authority in their postures unmistakable.

The man who spoke lifted a badge. "Agent Martino, FBI. We need you to come with us."

I widened my eyes. No one had called me by my *full* given name in a year. "How—"

"I'll explain everything in a minute. Let's go." The agent nodded toward a black town car idling by the curb and reached for me.

I jerked away from his grasp. "No. I have to get Kate. She's here."

He lifted an eyebrow. "You mean Kate Lewis, your wife?"

Before I could explain that she was in grave danger, shots rang out. Screams echoed down the street, too many of them at once to distinguish one as Kate's.

My whole body jolted forward, my heart beating like a jackhammer in my chest. Two more quick shots and more screams.

Kate. My God. Where was she? Adrenaline surged through my veins as a wave of people came rushing toward us, running away from the danger. I lurched toward it when a strong hand grabbed me and held me back.

"Not so fast, Lewis," the agent said. "You need to stay back with us."

I tried to rip away, but then all three of them were on me, halting my forward movement.

"Get off me!" I fought with all my might, but they'd taken me down to the ground. "Kate's over there. I need to get to her. She's not safe."

"Stop fighting, Lewis, goddamnit," another agent spoke through gritted teeth as he tried to hold me still.

No. I'd never stop fighting to protect her. I wrested one arm free and slugged the first face I saw. Agent Martino.

"Fuck!" He fell back, his hand over his eye.

Before I used the opportunity to escape, something hard came down on my head. The pain was blinding, piercing through my desperate determination.

In mere seconds, everything went black, and the sounds of chaos all around us drifted away.

♦ ♦ ♦ ♦

My body burned. Waves of heat singed my skin like the sun. The unrelenting island sun. Bright white light filled the frame of my vision, fading enough that I recognized the familiar landscape of Leiloa.

What was I doing here?

The rhythm of rough ocean waves crashed along the shore.

Stretches of beach that had come to feel like home sprawled all around me. Except this felt more like a desert to die in. My mouth was dry, my throat parched. My limbs didn't want to move.

Then I heard my name on her lips. Soft, like the song of a bird in the distance. I heard it again, stronger this time. I closed my eyes, wrapping every thought around the sound, as if I could draw her near with my mind.

Then I felt her. Cool palms sliding over my bare torso. She hovered above me like an angel from heaven. I blinked my eyes open, feeling my chest collapse with a whoosh.

Kate. My angel.

"Baby," I whispered, my throat seemingly healed by her mere presence.

She smiled sweetly, leaning forward to brush her lips over mine. I savored the soft touch only a moment before lifting into it, seeking more of her delicious mouth. I kissed her like a dying man, and she was shade and water. My only hope. Salvation on the edge of an unforgiving sea.

She straddled me slowly. She trailed her fingertips down my chest, and her breasts spilled free from her sheer white dress designed to tease rather than conceal. I covered their perfect softness with my hands, no longer dead weight, seemingly reawakened by the intense magnetic force that existed between our two bodies. How was it possible to crave her flesh like I did? I squeezed and pinched her nipples firmly. She closed her eyes with a breathy sigh, and my question floated away with the breeze.

She swiveled her hips, grinding against my groin. I drifted my palms from her breasts to the tops of her thighs, inching the delicate white fabric up until I could see her bare cunt. Before I could maneuver her onto my aching cock, she grabbed it, stroking from base to tip. I lifted my hips into every stroke. Then she shimmied lower, a coy smile curving her lips.

"Let me take care of you."

I groaned, because she hadn't stopped stroking me. And because I couldn't ignore the soul-deep ache to possess her fully, to feel her perfect pussy gloving me in this moment. But before I could argue for that, her lips were around me. Her tongue trailed perfect circles around my cock, swirling around the tip where she licked and sucked.

Perfection. Her mouth. Her body. Every succulent inch of her...

◆ ◆ ◆ ◆

"Lewis!"

The pleasure and the fantasy abruptly ended at the sound of my name echoing harshly off the walls. I blinked awake with a grimace, finding myself in a small shadowed room. The silhouette of a man caught my eye. I turned, but the small movement invited a bullet of pain shooting through my head, so violent that I immediately rolled off the bed and vomited in a nearby toilet.

Then I remembered everything. Someone had clocked me. Probably with his sidearm. The gates of what I identified now as a cell rolled open, and every movement of metal on metal seemed to reverberate in my brain. Without a doubt, I'd sustained a concussion from the blow. But even through the pain and the sickness, only one thought was truly clear.

I glanced up at the beefy guard. "Where's Kate?"

He shrugged. "Agent Martino is waiting for you. He's got the answers if there are any. Get up, kid."

I wiped my mouth and got to my feet. He led me to another room where, as promised, Agent Martino stood.

A deep purple bruise marked his cheekbone. He shot me a tight smile. "Lewis. We meet again. How are you feeling?"

Truthfully, I felt like I could probably use a doctor, and no matter how much trouble I was in, I should be entitled to one. But I only had one goal. One gnawing fear that penetrated the pain and my foggy brain.

"Where's Kate? She could still be with them. Did you look for her?" I couldn't hide the raw desperation in my voice.

Martino's expression didn't change. "Sit down."

I hesitated a moment before dropping into a chair. He sat across from me, his body crooked, his arm slung casually off the back of his chair. I resisted the urge to roll my eyes at the over-confident tough guy routine.

"You said you'd explain everything," I began.

"Then you fucking slugged me. What the hell?"

I slammed my fists on the table. "Do you know where my wife is or not?"

He shook his head, and my heart beat so loudly I barely heard his next words.

"You're going to tell me everything you know, Lewis. And then I'll tell you where your wife is."

My jaw fell a fraction and I snapped it shut. I wanted to slug him again and tell him precisely where he could shove his FBI power trip. But what could I do when I was this hopeless, not knowing where she was or if she was safe?

"We've been tailing you for a few weeks," he said. "You're slippery. I'll give you that."

I winced. "You've been tailing *me*?"

"Sure. We hung on the outskirts of the property you were staying at in Leiloa. We just watched, hoping your wife would lead us to whoever you guys are working for."

"Working for? What the hell are you taking about?"

"Cybermark Enterprises. Ring any bells?"

My jaw tightened.

"See, Lewis, I've been working this Cybermark case since before you fell off the map. People in their accounting department have been dropping like flies."

"I know."

"We figured you did. Or at least we thought your wife did. We followed a few tips that led us to your friends, Sven and Krister. We weren't too surprised to find them headquartered next to your old apartment. I can tell you we were pretty fucking surprised to find you alive on an island in the Pacific, though."

"Those blond hitmen are *not* my fucking friends. They've been stalking Kate ever since I reached out to her again."

"Is that so? You want to explain why you faked your own death if you have nothing to do with these murders?"

My lips fell agape. How could this be happening? How could they have it so wrong?

"They tried to kill me."

He lifted an eyebrow.

"I had been following their company through my work and noticed some odd numbers. I couldn't help myself. I wanted to dig deeper, so I reached out. They invited me to their headquarters in Switzerland and then put me on a goddamn death trap plane."

"The pilot's body was found. No trace of yours."

I shrugged. "One parachute."

He nodded.

"I didn't have anything to do with this. I..." I rubbed my forehead, unable to allay the physical or emotional pain that coursed through me. "I couldn't stay away from Kate anymore. I made a decision. Still not sure if it was the right one. But I couldn't live without her another day, at least not until she'd had a chance to decide whether to come live off the grid with me."

Agent Martino leaned in, pulled out a small notepad and pen from his jacket, and tapped the tip of the pen on the paper. "Let's start with what you know about Cybermark."

I shook my head even though it hurt to do so. "I'm not sure I know any more than you do. I have a history of financials that don't add up and a list of dead accountants."

He dropped his pen and pinched the bridge of his nose. "You're going to need more than that to get out of this. You faked your death, and you're in possession of falsified identification. Your wife collected on your life insurance. That's fraud. These are felonies we're talking about."

The list of offenses Martino ticked off meant so much to him and so little to me.

"These men are killing people! I faked my death to protect my wife. They would have killed us both. Jesus, they still want to. By some miracle, I survived a plane crash that should have killed me. I spent a few months doing manual labor, and after that, I bought a boat, taught myself to fish, and debated whether or not to risk Kate's life by reaching out to her. Whatever they're involved in, it has nothing to do with me. I swear to you."

A knock sounded at the door. Agent Martino rose, opened the door a crack, and spoke in a hushed whisper to whoever was outside. He poked his head back into the room. "I'll be back. We're not finished."

I rose quickly. "Where's Kate? You promised you'd tell me."

"You haven't told me everything."

"She's my goddamn wife! Tell me where she is!" My voice echoed loudly against the walls. My skin chilled with fear of the unknown. She could be in danger, or hurt. Who had fired the shots on the street? Had she found her way to safety? God help me, she could still be on the run. Or worse, she could be dead at the hands of those blond brothers, and these suits were just holding out to get more information from me before my whole world shattered.

Martino ignored my shouting and ducked away. I sucked in a series of uneven breaths, but nothing could calm me down short of another whack to the head. I was going to hyperventilate at this rate. Fisting my shaking hands in my hair, I paced the room. I berated myself. I prayed. I tried like hell to put together a plan, but I had no idea what I could devise in my current state.

Then, mercifully, Martino returned. Some of his smugness had slipped away. In fact, he appeared downright disappointed, like someone had tossed his ice cream cone on the ground.

I halted and held his stare. Only then did I notice a manila envelope in his hand that hadn't been there before. "What's going on?"

"Have a seat."

"Tell me where my wife is." I balled my fists, entertaining a fleeting vision of using them to get the answers I needed.

He lifted a hand, as if to wave off my unspoken wish. "Kate is being held here at the station. She's fine."

The relief was so intense—like a sudden change in the pressure of my whole body—all I could do was drop back into the chair and cradle my face in my hands. *Thank God. Thank God...*

After a moment I lifted my gaze to the agent. "What about the shots? I heard shots fired."

He nodded. "We had one team on Sven, one of the brothers, and another on you. We took down their driver, and when Alejandro Dominguez pulled his firearm on our guys, he went down. He died from his injuries. The brothers were taken into custody. We found Kate after everything went down, on her way to find you. We questioned her while you were passed out."

"And?"

He shrugged, an almost bored expression flattening his already unremarkable features. "Her story checks out with yours."

Even as I buzzed with relief knowing Kate was safe, we weren't out of the woods yet. Not if Martino really believed I could somehow be involved in Cybermark's heinous assassination spree.

"What now? What do I need to do to convince you I wasn't in on this?"

He leaned in and opened his folder. "Don't have to. But I will need your cooperation in this case against Cybermark if you want to avoid jail time for the fake IDs."

I frowned. "I'll tell you everything I know. But what's changed?"

"My partner just finished up with Sven and Krister. Typically we can get someone to roll over to save his own ass. This worked out a little differently. Turns out the brothers are quite close. You know, when they're not sinking people to the bottom of a lake. They both offered to take the heat. Sang like canaries to save the other. Pretty adorable, actually."

"Will it be enough to take Cybermark down?"

He shrugged. "It's a start. We'll need to fit the rest of the pieces together with their help. And yours."

"When can I see Kate?"

He rolled his eyes with a loud sigh. "Jesus Christ. I can see why you crawled out of the grave to be with the woman."

"You have no idea."

I was relieved, sure, but nothing would be right until she was in my arms again. Until I could touch her and hold her. The urge to tell her how much I loved her again, to apologize for not being able to keep her safe twisted me up inside. I had failed her, but I never would again.

The agent pulled a tape recorder from his pocket and positioned it on the table between us. "All right, Lewis. You're going to tell me everything, from the first time you came to know about Cybermark all the way to them coming after you and Kate. I need to know everything if we're going to take these fuckers down."

"And then what?"

"Then you can see your bride and start to get your life back. How does that sound?"

I nodded toward the recorder. "Turn that thing on. Let's do this."

EPILOGUE

Kate

He always said I had the most beautiful blue eyes he'd ever seen...

Price feasted between my legs, sucking and tugging, until I exploded into my third orgasm. I cried out as the ocean breeze drifted through our large window, coating my flesh in a cool blanket.

My husband crawled up my body, his hard cock nudging my thigh, and took my lips as he thrust into me.

Completion.

Pure completion as I'd always known it with Price, but now it was even more profound after what we'd been through to be together.

Our kiss was fueled by passion and desire, but mostly by the love and trust we shared in abundance. He pumped into me, touching every nerve ending inside me, melding into my body as only he could.

When he finally broke the intense kiss, we were both panting, sweat dripping from his brow as he gazed into my eyes, his own dark and smoky with lust.

No. Love.

"I love you, Kate. My Kate," he said, huffing.

"I love you too, baby. Always."

He continued to slam into me, our lovemaking intense as ever, but something made it even more special tonight—something I'd tell him later.

I looked into his blazing eyes, our gazes never wavering, and wrapped my legs around his bronze, muscular body, trying to push him deeper and deeper into me. When he nudged my clit, I shattered into pure bliss, the climax taking me through the glorious green hills of beautiful Bali, our home now.

"That's it, sweetness," he groaned. "Come for me. Just like—Ah!" He thrust into me balls deep.

I felt every spasm of his cock as he filled me, every beat of his heart as our chests crushed together, every drip of perspiration from his body that I welcomed onto my own.

We stayed joined for a few timeless moments until he rolled over. I crawled into his arms, nestling my head into the crook of his shoulder. I fit so perfectly against him.

The breeze still whispered gently, tousling the curtains that surrounded the bed in our oceanside bungalow. Our home was small and cozy, with two bedrooms in addition to ours, a kitchen, and a living room. That was it. All we needed. All we wanted. Small enough that we'd always know where the other was. We'd both promised never to let the other out of our sight again if possible.

Time would heal some of those wounds, I knew. But for now, I was content to always know my husband was never farther than a room or two away.

I sat up. "Price."

"Yeah, baby?"

"Come outside with me. I have something to tell you." I stood, wrapped myself in a sarong, and then stepped outside on the lanai attached to our bedroom.

I smiled, hugging myself.

Life was good. Everyone who'd been a threat to us was either dead or behind bars. Price's parents were back home, and Michelle... I laughed aloud. We weren't sure where Michelle was at any given moment. She'd gone off on a romp with Otis after they'd answered all the FBI's questions. Daily texts assured us that she was fine and happy. Price was keeping in touch with Otis, making sure his sister was safe and taken care of. He'd finally stopped grunting whenever the young man's name—and we still weren't sure if it was his real name—was mentioned. I'd never figured Chelle for a cougar, but life had a way of throwing curveballs into the best-laid plans. Price and I understood that better than anyone.

Price joined me, wearing nothing but a pair of denim cutoffs. I couldn't help but gawk at my husband. We'd been together for what sometimes seemed like forever, and my heart still beat a little faster every time I looked at him. And I'd always look at him. See him. Never take him for granted. I'd spent a year of my life without him, long enough to know I didn't want to spend another microsecond in that situation. We'd been given a second chance at happiness. At love. I wasn't about to screw that up.

"It's a gorgeous evening," Price said.

I nodded, staring at the sapphire ocean before us, the honey-hued sand, the tangerine ball of the setting sun. The waves hit the shore in a natural synchrony, creeping toward our haven and then easing away.

"You had something to tell me, Kate?" he said.

I turned to him, taking his hands. "I do."

He smiled. "Don't keep me in suspense."

My nerves jumping a little, I rubbed circles into his palm as I looked toward the water. "Why aren't there any seagulls here?"

"Probably because there's no food for them." He brought my hand to his lips and kissed it. "But I doubt that's what you wanted to talk about."

I traced the outline of his gorgeous lips. I had no reason to be nervous. This was something we'd always wanted, something I'd feared had been denied me. I was elated. I wanted nothing more than to have Price's child. "I've tried to be a good wife, Price."

He gripped my shoulders, his gaze serious. "You've been the best wife, baby. Better than I've deserved sometimes."

"Thank you for that," I said. "Do you think...?" I took in a deep breath.

"Think what?"

I cupped his stubbled cheek. "Do you think I'll be a good mother?"

"Are you kidding? You'll be the— Wait. What?" He stumbled backward. "Are you sure?"

I nodded, joy filling me. "I sneaked into the pharmacy while we were on our errands today. I got a pregnancy test. I was a couple days late, so I—"

He grabbed me and crushed me to his hard chest. "This is the best news, baby. The best." He brought his mouth down on mine.

The sun continued its descent, and the waves sloshed upon the beach, their melody enveloping us.

And we kissed. For a long time.

MORE MISADVENTURES

ALSO AVAILABLE FROM
WATERHOUSE PRESS

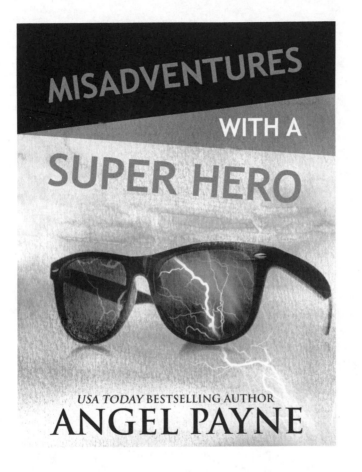

Keep reading for an excerpt!

PROLOGUE

REECE

She's got the body of a goddess, the eyes of a temptress, and the lips of a she-devil.

And tonight, she's all mine. In every way I can possibly fantasize.

And fuck, do I have a lot of fantasies.

Riveted by her seductive glance, I follow her into the waiting limo. A couple of friends from the party we've just left—their names already as blurry as the lights of Barcelona's Plaça Reial—swing hearty waves of departure, as if Angelique La Salle is taking me away on a six-month cruise to paradise.

Ohhh, yeah. I've never been on a cruise. As an heir to a massive hotel dynasty, I've never wanted for the utmost in luxurious destinations, but I've never been on a cruise. I think I'd like it. Nothing to think about but the horizon...and booze. Freedom from reporters, like the mob that were flashing their cameras in my face back at the club. What'll the headlines be, I wonder. Undoubtedly, they've already got a few combinations composed—a mix of the buzz words already trending about me this week. *Party Boy. Player. The Heir with the Hair. The Billionaire with the Bulge.*

Well. Mustn't disappoint them about the bulge.

And I sure as fuck don't plan to.

If my brain just happens to enjoy this as much as my body...I sure as hell won't complain.

Maybe she'll be the one.

Maybe she'll be...more.

The one who'll change things...at last.

As the driver merges the car into Saturday night traffic, Angelique moves her lush green gaze over everything south of my neck. Within five seconds my body responds. The fantasies in my brain are overcome by the depraved tempest of my body. My chest still burns from the five girls on the dance floor who group-hickied me. My shoulders are on fire from the sixth girl who clawed me like a madwoman while watching from behind. My dick pulses from a hard-on that won't stop because of the seventh girl—and the line of coke she snorted off it.

Angelique gazes at that part with lingering appreciation.

"*C'est magnifique.*" Her voice is husky as she closes in, sliding a hand into the open neckline of my shirt. Where's my tie? I was wearing one tonight—at some point. The Prada silk is long gone, much like my self-control. Beneath her roaming fingers, my skin shivers and then heats.

Well...shit.

Even if she's not going to be the one, she is at least *someone*. A body to warm the night. A presence, of *any* kind, to fill the depths. The emptiness I stopped thinking about a long damn time ago.

"You're magnificent too." I murmur, struggling to maintain control as she swings a Gumby-loose limb over my lap and straddles me. What little there is of her green cocktail dress rides up her thighs. She's wearing nothing underneath, of course—a fact that should have my cock much happier than it is. Troubling...but not disturbing. I'm hard, just not throbbing. Not *needing*. I'm not sure what I need anymore, only that I seem to spend a lot of time searching for it.

"So flawless," she croons, freeing the buttons of my shirt down to my waist. "*Oui.* These shoulders, so broad. This stomach, so etched. You are perfect, *mon chéri.* So perfect for this."

"For what?"

"You shall see. Very soon."

"I don't even get a hint?" I spread a smile into the valley between her breasts.

"That would take the fun out of the surprise, *n'est-ce pas*?"

I growl but don't push the point, mostly because she makes the wait well worth it. During the drive, she taunts and tugs, strokes and licks, teases and entices, everywhere and anywhere, until I'm damn near tempted to order the driver to pull over so I can pull out a condom and screw this temptress right here and now.

But where the hell is here?

Almost to the second I think the question, the limo pulls into an industrial park of some sort. A secure one, judging by the high walls and the rolling door that allows us to roll directly into the building.

Inside, at least in the carport, all is silent. The air smells like cleaning chemicals and leather...and danger. Nothing like a hint of mystery to make a sex club experience all the sweeter.

"A little trip down memory lane, hmmm?" I nibble the bottom curve of Angelique's chin. It's been three weeks since we'd met in a more intimate version of this type of place, back in Paris. I'd been hard-up, she'd been alluring. End of story. Or beginning, depending on how one looks at it. "How nostalgic of you, darling."

As she climbs from the limo, she leaves her dress behind in a puddle on the ground. It wasn't doing much good where I bunched it around her waist anyway. "Come, my perfect Adonis."

Perfect. I don't hear that word often, at least not referring to me. Too often, I'm labelled with one of those media favorites, or if I'm lucky, one of the specialties cooked up by Dad or Chase in their weekly phone messages. Dad's a little more lenient, going for shit like "hey, stranger" or "my gypsy kid." Chase doesn't pull so many punches. Lately, his favorite has been "Captain Fuck-Up."

"Bet *you'd* like to be Captain Fuck-Up right about now, asshole," I mutter as two gorgeous women move toward me, summoned by a flick of Angelique's fingers. Their white lab coats barely hide their generous curves, and I find myself taking peeks at their sheer white hose, certain the things must be held up by garters. Despite the kinky getups, neither of them crack so much as a smile while they work in tandem to strip me.

I'm so caught up in what the fembots are doing, I've missed Angelique putting on a new outfit. Instead of the gold stilettos she'd rocked at the club, she's now in sturdier heels and a lab coat. Her blonde waves are pulled up and pinned back.

"Well, well, well. Doctor La Salle, I presume?" Eyeing her new attire with a wicked smirk, I ignore the sudden twist in my gut as she sweeps a stare over me. Her expression is stripped of lust. She's damn near clinical.

"Oh, I am not a doctor, *chéri.*"

I arch my brows and put both hands on my hips, strategically guiding her sights back to my jutting dick. I may not know how the woman likes her morning eggs yet, but I *do* know she's a sucker for an arrogant bastard—especially when he's naked, erect, and not afraid to do something about it.

"Well, that's okay, *chérie*." I swagger forward. "I can pretend if you can."

Angelique draws in a long breath and straightens. Funny, but she's never looked hotter to me. Even now, when she really does look like a doctor about to lay me out with shitty test results. "No more pretending, *mon ami*."

"No more—" My stomach twists again. I glance backward. The two assistants aren't there anymore, unless they've magically transformed into two of the burliest hulks I've ever seen not working a nightclub VIP section.

But these wonder twins clearly aren't here to protect me.

In tandem, they pull me back and flatten me onto a rolling gurney.

And buckle me down. Tight.

Really tight.

"What. The. *Fuck*?"

"Sssshhh." She's leaning over my face—the wonder fuckers have bolted my head in too—brushing tapered fingers across my knitted forehead. "This will be easier if you don't resist, *mon trésor*."

"This? This...*what*?"

Her eyes blaze intensely before glazing over—with insanity. "History, Reece! We are making *history*, and you are now part of it. One of the most integral parts!"

"You're—you're batshit. You're not forging history, you bitch.

You're committing a crime. This is kidnapping!"

Her smile is full of eerie serenity. "Not if nobody knows about it."

"People are going to know if I disappear, Angelique."

"Who says you are going to disappear?"

For some reason, I have no comeback for that. No. I *do* know the reason. Whatever she's doing here might be insanity—but it's well-planned insanity.

Which means...

I'm screwed.

The angel I trusted to take me to heaven has instead handed me a pass to hell.

Making this, undoubtedly, the hugest mess my cock has ever gotten me into.

This story continues in Misadventures of a Super Hero!

```
TELL THE WORLD THIS BOOK WAS

GOOD    |    BAD    |    SO-SO
```

ABOUT MEREDITH WILD

Meredith Wild is a #1 *New York Times, USA Today,* and international bestselling author of romance. Living on Florida's Gulf Coast with her husband and three children, she refers to herself as a techie, whiskey-appreciator, and hopeless romantic. She has been featured on *CBS This Morning, The Today Show,* the *New York Times, The Hollywood Reporter, Publishers Weekly,* and *The Examiner.*

VISIT HER AT MEREDITHWILD.COM!

ABOUT HELEN HARDT

#1 New York Times, #1 USA Today, and #1 Wall Street Journal Bestselling author Helen Hardt's passion for the written word began with the books her mother read to her at bedtime. She wrote her first story at age six and hasn't stopped since. In addition to being an award winning author of contemporary and historical romance and erotica, she's a mother, a black belt in Taekwondo, a grammar geek, an appreciator of fine red wine, and a lover of Ben and Jerry's ice cream. She writes from her home in Colorado, where she lives with her family. Helen loves to hear from readers.

VISIT HER AT HELENHARDT.COM!